SILENCER

A Novella

Julie Roberts Towe

ISBN: 978-0-9908007-5-0 (paperback)

ISBN: 978-0-9908007-4-3 (ebook)

This book is a work of fiction. All names, characters, places, organizations, businesses and events other than those clearly in the public domain are used fictitiously and are the product of the author's imagination. Any resemblance to actual events, locales, or persons, living or dead, is entirely coincidental.

Stitched Wing Publishing
1719 Angel Parkway, Ste. 400-116
Allen, TX 75002
USA

Cover art and design by Mr. Brown

For Moose, Jake, Jason, & Woody.

I love you all.

1

Rhoda pressed the left side of her face firmly into the dry dirt between the pumpkin vines. She pressed with such force that she could no longer discern the grainy texture of the soil. She thought the ground might keep her brain from making too much mess when she pulled the trigger. She thought a lot of other things, too. Thoughts swirled in her head like a tornado of images, sensations, flashes of memory, smells, sounds, so much.

She breathed in deeply. The smell of the soil changed as flecks of dirt warmed inside her nostrils to become heavy scents full of death. She opened her eyes, tears set loose to roll over the edge of her nose and into her other eye. Her brain latched onto the sensation of cold tears falling into her warm eye, blending with new warm tears. The distraction offered her a moment to take in the view. From her angle, she could only see beneath the giant pumpkin leaves cupped up to catch the sun. Nearly all the pumpkins were gone. Vines snaked about like mothers' arms reaching for babies. She closed her eyes, took a breath of air, and held it for a moment before letting it out in a slobbery silent sob. The pain pulled her back into the unbearable whirlwind growing inside herself.

She raised the pistol, thinking she should have probably brought a shotgun for better outcome, but at least the pistol would not break her head apart. Rhoda only wanted the bullet to snip into her brain, disconnect it from her senses, kill the noise. She imagined the coming bang and the following silence, desperately wanting the silence to come. She told herself it was time, allowed her brain to study the thought of the bang, study it one last time, drink a gluttonous fill of thought, then she would do it.

Rhoda maneuvered the pistol along the back of her neck, contemplating where, exactly, to aim. Her mind spun in a maelstrom of information: where the bullet should hit, how to get it there, cautionary tales not to screw it up. The spinning increased to the point she thought she would pass out and fail to go through with it at all. Her heart rate sped out of control; her stomach tightened. She was terrified.

"Damn it," she whispered and forced her thoughts back to the funeral. The white open casket had been beautiful, but she had wanted ashes. She wished she had them to hold now. But they had said it wasn't proper to burn the child.

Rhoda's sorrow began to swallow up her fear (as she

had intended). Now was the time. She breathed her lungs full of air and held her breath again. Her finger steadied on the trigger. Her lungs begged to exhale and breathe again, but she held it in, her ears ringing in beautiful distraction. "I'm so sorry," she thought to no one, there was no one to truly care. With eyes squinted tight, lungs burning, face red and sweating, she tightened the muscles of her arm to hold their position and counted back from three, two, one.

An unexpected pain shot over her hand and arm before the gunshot fired. In her confusion, she heard the bullet hit the ground ten feet in front of her.

"What in the hell you doing on my land?" The deep voice exploded above her. Someone clutched her throbbing hand which still held the gun. Rhoda rolled onto her back and looked up to see the the silhouette of a tall, broad shouldered, Black man with a head so big it made Rhoda respect the man's mother for having birthed him. He was seething angry. He said, "Did those Crosswhites send your sorry ass up here to cause me more trouble? You people are like damn roaches, come crawling out in droves when times are darkest. I'd let you go on and kill yourself for being such a fool, but I ain't accounting for the death of you. They damn sure aren't accounting for the death of my wife."

Rhoda noticed he was carrying a shotgun, the kind she knew would work best for suicide. She considered telling him she had chosen the pistol so as not to leave much mess, but decided it best to say nothing. Surely he would let her go and she could find another place.

While her mind busied itself with thinking of alternative options and places to go, his other hand snatched her pistol away. "I can not believe you people," he shook his head as he removed the bullets one by one, "Your harassment knows no bounds. You come up here to kill yourself, like what do you even care if I'm here if you're dead? Are you worried next year I might plant twice as many pumpkins and shear double the amount of sheep? You worried I'm going to get twice as full of my Black self?"

"I don't know you," Rhoda squinted hard to make out his features in the shadow of the low evening sun setting behind him.

"Damn right, you don't. Now get off my property." He turned and began walking away with Rhoda's gun in one hand and his shotgun in the other.

She sat up. "Wait! I'll go, but I need my gun!" She got on her knees and frantically moved her hands around in the dirt until she managed to find four bullets. She only needed one. She stood up and slid the bullets into her coat pocket. Then she ran to catch up to the man, realizing just how out of shape she had become. Her knees wobbled a little and the flesh on her arms and back moved in a way it never used to move. Images of high school flashed into her mind, tight waisted dresses, dances, boys wrapping arms around her, feeling beautiful and wanted. Now she felt like she was neither. Hurtful and self-loathing thoughts radiated through her brain like buckshot. She mentally pleaded with it to shut up, just shut up. "I need my gun!" She grabbed the man's arm.

He jerked his arm away from her, but he stopped walking. She stood beside him, bent over, breathing hard, not wanting to look into his eyes. She saw the tips of his boots move as he turned toward her.

He watched her gasping for air. "You should try to do some work sometime, get up off the couch and plant something, do something useful."

She raised her head enough to see he had tightened his grip on her pistol. His hand was nearly as large as the gun. There would be no way to fight him for it. But maybe if she fought him, he would shoot her. It would save her the trouble.

"You're not getting it back," he interrupted her thoughts. "I'm about a ten minute walk from home. When I get there, I'm calling the police. They won't give a shit about my situation, but maybe they'll haul your ass off for your own good. You can follow me around like a dog 'til then, or you can go willingly before they get here so you can get your life the hell back together."

"I need my gun." Rhoda pleaded. She finally looked up into his eyes, only because it was her last hope. They were big, chestnut colored eyes. Beneath his eyes, his cheeks were covered with freckles. His face had the beginnings of a stubbly beard which may have been due to neglect or the coming winter. She couldn't tell which. For all the anger and annoyance in his voice, there wasn't an ounce of it discernible from his expression. He just looked tired, mentally and emotionally. Physically, however, he looked able to fight off a grizzly. She tried to assess his state of mind, but it was impossible.

"What you need this for?" He rotated his hand which held the gun and gave a hard stare into her eyes.

"I…" she couldn't possibly say the truth aloud, even though he already knew the answer. "It belonged to my grandmother." She hoped that bit of truth would be enough.

"So you plan to treasure it for all your life? The life you plan on ending on my property?"

"Please?" She begged, holding out her hand, sweaty

palm up. Tears began to burn her eyes.

"I don't want your blood on my hands," he said, less angry. "I am not giving you the gun. I am not having you die on my land. I am not having anything to do with this other than walking back to my house, calling the police, and handing them this tiny little woman gun. What makes you think this thing would even work, anyway? You'd have shot yourself and been paralyzed, disfigured, looking like a monster the rest of your life. If you're hellbent on dying, you better think of a better way. You can think on it while you're headed west, or east, or go the fuck north where you'll eventually die of hypothermia over the holidays. I don't care where you go, but you have got to go and get off my property."

2

She followed him, two steps behind, her eyes on the pistol in his hand. Her tired feet throbbed with every step. She was exhausted in so many ways. All she wanted was to sleep, forever.

Her mind wondered back in time as if half in a dream. She remembered the moment she decided to not look back. She had dragged the wooden chair from the kitchen to the hall closet. She had climbed up with creaky knees groaning and reached for the box on the top shelf. That was the box her grandmother had made up for her, sealed, and designated Rhoda's by will. Out of six grandchildren, Rhoda had been the only one to get a box. She had also been the only one not included in the divvying of monetary inheritance. Five grandchildren received $113.72 each. They all stared at Rhoda's box as if what was inside would indicate if Grandma Vickers loved Rhoda more than them, even though they all knew the truth was that she didn't.

When Rhoda had pulled the box from the closet and opened it, the feeling that came over her was just as it was the first time she had broken the seal in front of her cousins. Inside was a small porcelain figurine of a baby lying in the curve of a sickle moon, a kitchen towel wrapped around it to keep it from breaking. Beside it was the antique pistol. The sound of her cousins murmuring had stayed with Rhoda. She heard them all over again when she opened the box in the privacy of her own home.

She pictured her grandmother smiling over her now, watching Rhoda trudge through the tall dry grass of a field in the middle of nowhere. She felt Grandma Vickers watch her, but knew it was not quite joyously that she did so. Rhoda clearly saw her nod, knowingly, to say this moment was planned long ago. It was as if that moment had been predicted, Rhoda would shoot herself. Rhoda would be pushed over the edge and would need to end her misery. Grandma Vickers had known and had provided the means.

Surely Rhoda's conclusion was preposterous. But that's what Rhoda's mind did to things. It would start with one small sad thought. That sad thought would turn into a black hole, pulling in more and more terrible imaginings. Eventually, even the good thoughts turned sour and spun into the spiral toward darkness. All of Rhoda's life, she had fought it. But now it was winning and she was okay to let it win.

She hadn't been the only one to give up. When her husband, Ed, had driven off the Kyle's Ford Bridge with

Olivia on his lap, he had given up for the both of them. The Buick had landed upside down in the river, Ed's body trapped inside it; but Olivia's body had floated downstream. Her tiny pink onesie caught on a branch and held her face down in the water for twelve hours before anyone had found her. Rhoda's mind now clung to the memory that Olivia had lost a shoe. It was one of the shoes Rhoda had purchased on the day she had found out she was pregnant. She had been so excited and terrified to think she was going to be a mother. She hadn't been sure if she could do it. She still wasn't sure if she could be a mother, or even if she had at all, having been a mother for such a short period of time before Olivia's death. All of her worries and preparations to raise her daughter to have a better life than her own had come to naught. Nothing had mattered in the end. Ed had taken everything that had finally made Rhoda want to live.

While her mind scanned over her memories, Rhoda walked all the way to the man's house without knowing how she had gotten there, or how she hadn't fallen over a vine or tripped over a rock. She just came out of her memories and there she was, standing in the yard of a house so old, whoever built it had probably rode in on a wagon. The two story farmhouse was painted a pale yellow. Bright yellow mums grew in blue ceramic flowerpots by the front stairs. An antique horse plow rusted in a nearby flowerbed surrounded by pansies and loose pumpkins for decoration. For a moment, Rhoda forgot everything. The house itself seemed to generate waves of invisible memories all its own, thoughts she could not grasp, but could feel to her bones.

While she stood blinking in the yard, the man disappeared into the house. The slam of the screen door snapped her out of her trance just enough to remember why she had followed him. Her gun. She darted into the house where the sound of a screaming infant caused her heart to nearly implode.

"That's not Olivia," she told herself, but it did little to quell her panic. The screams were desperate, full of pain and longing, a child on the brink of insanity. Why had the man left his baby alone? Rage filled Rhoda to overflowing. Even she was surprised by the intensity of her response. She wanted to make him pay for the pain she heard in the child's cry. Again, she reminded herself the cries were not Olivia's. The man was not Ed. But she was still angry and a part of her felt guilty. If he had not been busy saving Rhoda's life, he would have been there for his child. She was partly to blame.

The whirring of rage slowly turned to the stillness of contemplation as she stood in the living room, hearing the crying, smelling beef stew. Her eyes focused on the wall of framed portraits against a backdrop of opalescent wallpaper with images of turquoise flowers vining upward in wispy columns. She felt pulled to take a closer look at each portrait. At any other time, perhaps she would have. But she was pulled with a greater force toward the urgent cries of the child. Without having a clear plan, she followed her instinct and stepped one foot in front of the other until she reached the kitchen where a bassinet had been set by the table. The baby inside it kicked and punched into the air. Rhoda walked closer and looked down at her, a baby girl in a white sleeper covered with yellow stars. The baby's eyes were squinted closed where pools of tears accumulated before slipping off down toward her ears, her mouth contorted open in a wail.

"Who are you?" A woman's voice caused Rhoda to jump. She turned to see a short, frail Black woman wearing a lime green and teal head wrap. Her knobby arthritic hand was raised with one finger pointing shakily at Rhoda. Her black eyes held a curious spark.

"I'm Rhoda."

"Did you come to help with the baby?" The older woman smiled. "Ms. Cutshire said she would find someone, as if she hadn't done enough by sending over stew and adding us to the prayer list. Thank you so much for coming, dear." She reached into the bassinet with her trembling hands and lifted out the crying girl with such unsteadiness that Rhoda feared the child would be dropped. Rhoda quickly reached over to help, taking the baby into her own arms. The child had nearly lost its voice from screaming, yet she continued to punch her small brown fists and kick strong little legs.

As soon as Rhoda had the baby tucked comfortingly in her arms, the child turned her head toward the direction of Rhoda's breast. With open mouth rummaging around the front of her coat, the infant frantically searched for something to suck. Not finding it, the child's mouth turned down in heartbreak as it began to wail again.

"She's hungry," Rhoda whispered to herself before looking to the woman in confusion. How could this child be so hungry if someone had been with her all along, able to feed her at any time?

"She's having a hard time," the woman explained, holding a shaking finger out to the child's mouth for it to suck. The baby girl latched on and sucked the finger only a few seconds before becoming wise to the trick and crying again. The woman continued, "No child should lose their mother so early."

"Lose?" Rhoda knew what that normally meant, yet it still took her a moment to recall the man saying something about the death of his wife. She barely registered it at the time, hearing it as an abstract concept in the background of her incessant brain-chatter. Now, it hit her hard in the stomach.

"I know I should call it what it was, murder," the woman shivered, "But I don't like to say it in front of the child." The woman turned and walked toward the stove, "I'm warming her a bottle, but she won't take it. Everyone who has tried has failed. Maybe she will take it from you. Surely she won't keep starving herself."

With the bottle in hand, Rhoda took a seat in a wooden kitchen chair. She tried again and again to coax the little girl's lips to latch onto the bottle. The baby jerked her head away in alarm and disgust, wailing as the drops of formula accumulated on her tongue, unswallowed, until she began to gag. Rhoda quickly held her upright and wiped her mouth with a towel. She felt her own hands begin to shake; frustration and self-loathing washed over her. She was a terrible mother, an absolute failure.

A thought entered her mind; there was one last thing to try, something which Rhoda suspected would take every last ounce of her own sanity to attempt. But how could she deny this child what was desperately needed?

"I have milk," Rhoda said as her heart tightened into a painful ball. Her tears stung as they began to fill her eyes. "I can feed her." The tears spilled over and ran down her cheeks. She wiped at them with the towel, smearing formula across her face. The stench nearly made her gag, too. No wonder the child didn't want to drink that foul smelling liquid.

"You're a wet nurse?" The old woman covered her gaping mouth as her eyes sparkled with hope. "Oh, our prayers are answered!"

"I... I'm not a wet nurse." Rhoda's tears fell onto the baby, "It's just that... my child is dead."

"I am so sorry," the old woman grabbed hold of the back of a chair to support herself. Feeling unsettled, she carefully lowered herself into the seat. "This is a terrible world. It must have taken everything you had to come here for little Nanshe."

Rhoda nodded, letting the old woman believe whatever she must. The only thing Rhoda cared about was stopping the baby's pain. She handed the child back to the old woman. Nanshe's screams increased in volume despite the cracking and hoarseness of her tiny voice. Rhoda unbuttoned and urgently pulled off her coat before slinging it haphazardly onto the floor. She took Nanshe back into her arms, balancing her carefully as she raised her sweater and offered the child her breast, uncertain if her milk would come.

Nanshe latched on and sucked voraciously. Rhoda's skin felt the physical pain followed by the sensation of her milk letting down. Then came the lump in her throat caused by the onslaught of hormones, and lastly, the uncaged emotion of her broken heart. She, not Nanshe, threw back her head and wailed with despair. Tears ran from her upturned eyes, down the sides of her face, and into her ears.

"Oh, God!" She cried to a deity in which she had lost all faith.

"I will help you," said the old woman. Rhoda heard the chair legs scrape the floor as the woman rose from it. The sound of the soles of her shoes on the wooden floor moved farther away until the woman's voice called out from the hall, "Benoni! Come!"

3

The woman shuffled back to the stove and hurriedly filled a teapot with water. Ben's heavy footsteps made their way down the hall and stopped at the doorway. The woman spoke loudly to be heard over Rhoda's wails, "I am making her chamomile tea to calm her. Take the blanket from the bassinet. Help her hold Nanshe so she will not drop her."

Ben looked at Rhoda's hand, the red and bruised hand he had just kicked in the pumpkin patch. It now cradled the head of his daughter; it was the only still and steady part of an otherwise tremulous body. Rhoda sobbed with her face turned up to the ceiling. She didn't see Ben, and her cries were so loud that she likely did not hear him. He worried he would go to wrap Nanshe in the blanket and scare the woman into dropping his daughter. He knew by the way Rhoda's fingers gently cupped his daughter's skull that she would not drop her.

"Why do you not do as I say?" The old woman screamed at him as if he were a child. "You have lost Della. Do you wish to lose your Nanshe, too?"

"I did not lose her," His voice held a forced calm that barely rose above the sound of Rhoda's cries. The steady tone of it caught Rhoda's ear and caused her to raise her head to see him standing before her. She tugged at her sweater to hide her breast, not because it was a breast, but because his own daughter was latched there without his permission.

Ben lifted a yellow knitted blanket from the bassinet and tossed it so that it landed draped over Rhoda's shoulder, hiding his daughter's face. He continued his forced and steady tone as he spoke to the old woman, "They took her from me, Paumina. They take whatever they want."

As his eyes rested on Rhoda, they gave no sign of the pain inside of him. Paumina brought Rhoda chamomile tea in a pale green teacup with pink and coral roses swirling and twisting beneath the rim. Rhoda stared at it, distracted again by the feel of Nanshe's rhythmic sucking and her tiny fist pressed against Rhoda's heart. She thought it would be easy to close her eyes and imagine Nanshe was Olivia. She could, for a moment, live as though the nightmare had never happened. She could pretend she and Olivia were visiting friends, just having tea in the kitchen of a kind old woman as Olivia finished up her last feeding before they headed back home. Even with her eyes open, Rhoda could still feel the fantasy so distinctly that it transformed the room.

"You should go home, Paumina," said Ben. "You haven't rested for days."

"I had planned to miss church tomorrow, but I would like to go if you are sure you can manage Nanshe alone."

"I am not alone. Now go. You never miss church."

Paumina glanced at Rhoda, noticing how she sat like a statue except for one of her fingers which repeatedly flicked into the teacup handle and then out again. Ben had said he was not alone, but Paumina felt he most certainly was. She didn't feel right leaving and opened her mouth to offer once more to stay. But Ben cut her off with a firm command.

"Go."

All she could do was nod nervously as she retrieved her long beige coat and her black leather purse from the coat rack by the door. She exited out the back and soon the sound of an engine could be faintly heard. Rhoda continued to fondle the teacup as if her fingers were in need of touch more than her mouth needed to drink. When the car had driven away and the room fell silent, Ben cleared his throat.

"Where is your child?" He asked with accusation.

"My child is buried in Lawson Cemetery, a two mile flight on the back of a black bird from the river where her body was found." Rhoda tapped the rim of the teacup with her fingernail, felt the tears slipping over her cheeks again, but she had no energy left to truly cry.

"What happened to her?" Ben was still skeptical, not entirely convinced Rhoda had not caused the death.

"My husband drove off the bridge. He left a note, said he couldn't let her live and couldn't live with himself for killing her. One week ago today, everything I had to live for died. So, anytime you would like to give me my gun, I'll be out of your way."

Ben reached into the inside pocket of his jacket and pulled out her gun. Rhoda's eyes widened as if seeing a long lost love. Ben opened the cylinder to ensure the bullets had been removed, popped it closed and set it on the table out of her reach. With his finger pressed to the table through the trigger guard, he began to spin the pistol around like a top. He watched Rhoda with both curiosity and disdain. "How can you have thoughts of killing yourself while a baby nurses life from your breast?"

"I'm not heartless. My heart feels for this child as it did for Olivia. If I closed my eyes now, it would be like I was back home before she died. If I could keep them closed forever, the pain would end. But I have to open my eyes sometime. The only way to keep them closed forever is to die."

Ben looked away as his mind reflected on the first sight of Rhoda's white breast. He had been shocked, momentarily unable to comprehend why Della's breast was white. Now, he tried to imagine Della was the one sitting before him, feeding Nanshe, but he could no long conjure up the illusion. There was no reprieve for his pain and he envied this stranger.

"What's your name?" He asked her.

"Rhoda Evanson," she sniffed and sat up straight as if suddenly remembering she was in a stranger's home.

"Rhoda Evanson," Ben repeated and gave the gun a spin again. "You know, I already called the police." He watched Rhoda squirm a little as a look of shame washed over her. "I said, 'I found a White woman on my property with a gun saying she was going to shoot herself. I told her to head on out of here, but you might want to check on her.' Do you want to guess what the officer told me?"

22

Rhoda shook her head, nervous but distracted by the feel of Nanshe drifting into deep sleep and letting loose her hold. Rhoda reached under the yellow blanket to pull her sweater down. She began to wrap Nanshe in the blanket as Ben answered his own question.

"They told me, 'Boy, you better hope we don't find you in trouble with no White woman. Just because you blame those Crosswhite boys for what happened to your wife don't mean you can take it out on one of ours.' And then he laughed, the son of bitch. There's nothing ever going to change when every officer in Grand Saline is a card carrying member of the KKK."

"I'm not from here," Rhoda explained defensively, "I rode the buses as far from Tennessee as I could afford to go, then I walked as far as my legs would carry me. I don't even know where I am right now, much less anything about the Crosswhite boys. But, I know I'm not like them. It don't mean much to you, I know. But I ain't prejudice."

Ben threw back his head and laughed causing Nanshe to startle but not quite enough to wake her completely. Rhoda tucked Nanshe's tiny arms back into the blanket and wrapped it tighter. Ben said, "No, ya'll never are. You love Blacks. But you don't do a thing about those who hate us, do you? Turn a blind eye to the whole damn business."

"I'm not from here," Rhoda said again as her face burned from the discomfort his words were causing.

"Well, welcome to Grand Saline, Texas! You are in the thick of it now. The question has become, how do I get you out of here without getting arrested or strung up?"

"I didn't mean to make trouble for you," Rhoda stood and slowly shuffled over to the bassinet where she laid Nanshe on her back. The blanket stayed in place, swaddling Nanshe so tightly she never realized she had been put down. Rhoda nodded satisfactorily at her accomplishment.

Then she eyed the gun on the table. She tensed with adrenaline and stood motionless behind Ben. She wanted to take it, but couldn't figure out how to get away with it. She breathed a deep, steady breath and exhaled her resignation, then went back to sit in the kitchen chair where she had been. She picked up her cup of tea. "Can you just drive me to the next town over?"

"Hell naw! You are not getting in my truck." Ben pushed his palms against his closed eyelids and then ran his fingers up over his short hair.

"Why do you live here if it's so hard? Why not move?" Rhoda asked, thinking of Mr. Hughes, the only Black man in the War Gap community, probably the only Black man within fifteen miles of it. She had always wondered if he was happy there, but hadn't known him well enough to ask.

"Okay," sighed Ben, "I'll tell you a story if you want to know. It's been on my mind anyway, like it needs me to say it aloud because there's something in it I need to understand. I need to take a good look at it in light of all that's happened. With Della."

Rhoda nodded and took a sip of the tea.

4

Ben walked to the stove and ladled out two bowls of beef stew. He sat one by Rhoda and the other at his place. He went to the fridge and poured himself a glass of iced tea. All the while, Rhoda's eyes followed him, catching sight of the kitchen window and the darkness which had fallen beyond it. When Ben returned to the table with his tea, he also brought a plate of biscuits from that morning's breakfast. When he sat them in the center of the table, he realized he had left the pistol unguarded and was surprised that Rhoda had not taken it. Confused, but determined not to show it, he slid the pistol back into the pocket inside his coat.

He sat, took a swallow of his tea, and began to tell the story of how he came to own a farm in Grand Saline,

Texas.

"Everyone around here thinks they know this story. And to them it's old news. But preparing to tell it to you makes me think of just how shocking some of this might be. But I need to tell it, so I will," He exhaled and shifted in his seat, "The man I was named after moved here in 1866 at the end of the war. He was a newly freed Black man. So why would he come to Texas? Well, let's back up a little. In the years of the war, he had been owned like a head of cattle by Nathaniel Whitmer who had two sons, Nate Jr. and Henry. They lived in Georgia. Nathaniel Sr. and Nate Jr. signed up with the Confederate Army and left Henry there to help his mother run the farm and switch from producing cotton to growing food. While Henry was preparing to grow corn and potatoes, Nate Jr. was getting himself killed in Gettysburg. Then a few years later word came that Nathaniel Sr. was killed in Chickamauga. The final blow came at the end of 1864 when General Sherman came through and burned down every damn thing. The soldiers had retrieved the horses from the stable and set loose the slaves, but they didn't bother to wake Mrs. Whitmer sleeping in her bed. Henry might have woken her to save her had he been home. But he had been out in the night tending to a personal matter with Benoni."

Ben paused to spoon up a bite of beef stew. He chewed it and hummed at its deliciousness before taking a swallow of tea. He didn't bother to look at Rhoda since he really didn't care what she thought of the tale. He was telling it for himself. "So, the war ended five months later and a number of things could have happened. Benoni was a free man and strong. He had been selling himself out for work since he was just fifteen. He could have gone north. So, why didn't he? I guess for the same reason Henry didn't rebuild in Georgia. He sold the land, and he and Benoni moved to Grand Saline. Henry bought 57 acres, 39 prairie grass, 18 wooded with post oak. Rumor has it that Henry and Benoni lived like man and wife and that their homosexual acts have cursed this land. But, there weren't no curses here. They had this house built up by 1870. They left prairie grass around the perimeter and it is now some of the last original prairie in Grand Saline. How'd they know to do that? I don't think they did. I think they expected trouble, sabotage, and kept a tract of land between themselves and the surrounding farms. And they didn't waste any time causing trouble of their own. They hired only Blacks and paid them high wages. They had no want for money; they farmed to feed themselves and others and to make good use of the land. Around here, that's what causing trouble looks like.

"And maybe you wonder how I came to be named after a gay man," Ben laughed and shook his head but still didn't look at Rhoda whom, for the first time in days, was not thinking about her life at all. "Well, in 1921 Henry dies and wills Benoni his half of the farm. A few years later, in 1924, Benoni's walking out through the field to check on a new family he had hired to shear sheep. They were living in the barn until they earned enough for rent somewhere else. Benoni hears arguing, goes up to look between the barn slats and sees the father slapping his daughter who ain't more than 15 years old. Benoni rushes into the barn about the time the father grabs the girl by her braided hair and yanks her down to her knees in front of him. That girl was Paumina, you should know. She told me this herself, so I know all this is true."

Ben took another couple of bites of stew, quickly chewing and swallowing so he could continue the story.

"Paumina's dad had always beaten her. But Benoni had been the first person to stand up for her. He told the old man he would give him a hundred dollars if he would leave his farm and never return, but Paumina must stay with him. The man jumped at the offer, but Paumina's mother cried. She told Paumina it was for the best, to be brave, and all that as if she had any true concern for her daughter's safety. But Paumina thinks her mother was just crying because she was shamed by Benoni's good heart.

"Benoni was 79 years old when he married 15 year old Paumina. Everyone thought of Benoni as a dirty old man, but Paumina says he asked nothing of her until he became too weak to feed and clean himself. He lived to be 90 years old and Paumina probably gave him the last four years just by taking good care of him. She loved him, for sure, like a father. When he died, he left it all to her.

"I call her my mother, but she is not. I am the son of one of the farm workers she hired to scour wool. Her name was Carper and Paumina never knew if that name was her first or last. She was a large woman and was not aware, or did not make known, she was pregnant when Paumina had hired her. Paumina found her after she had given birth, me in her arms. She was so weak from blood loss that she could not even hold open her eyes. She couldn't be saved, but I lived. Paumina kept me and named me Benoni Whitmer, and I became the first member of the third generation of unrelated kin.

"When I married Della two years ago in 1967, Paumina signed the farm over to us, said she was too old to work it and wanted to live in town by the church. She shares a house with Sister Brinley. But now she says she might move in here again, help with Nanshe. She says it's too much on one man to run a farm and raise a baby. But, I think she's worried they'll kill me."

Rhoda nearly choked on the tea she had been about to swallow. "But why would anyone kill you?" Her voice startled Ben. For a brief moment, he had forgotten she was there. But he didn't look at her upon remembering. He suspected she would have a look of pity on her face and that was the last thing he wanted to see.

He said, "Because I'm Black, ain't that enough?"

"No!" She breathed a half sigh and half grunt. "No, it isn't!"

"Well, makes no difference if you agree it's true or not. The Crosswhites own 47 acres to the west of me and another tract of 18 acres of cattle pasture to the north. Their youngest son is of marrying age and needs a place of his own. My land would be just about right."

Rhoda set her cup on the table and tried to think of something in her own life which might relate to Ben's story. "One time, in Tennessee, Mrs. Hawk's son was going to get married and she asked Mr. Diltner if she could buy a couple of acres of his mountain land so her son could build a little house up in there on the ridge. Mr. Diltner was a very old man and Mrs. Hawk thought he could use the money more than he could use that mountainside. But Mr. Diltner told her that land was set aside for his grandson and he wouldn't feel right about letting it go. Mrs. Hawk reluctantly pointed out to Mr. Diltner that his grandson had died in the Vietnam War. Mr. Diltner had forgotten that. He never could even remember what he ate for breakfast by lunchtime and was always needing to be reminded of things. But, when Mr.

Diltner heard again for what felt like the first time that his grandson was dead, even though a year had passed since the real first time, he almost fell over dead himself. Mrs. Hawk wished Mr. Diltner had fallen over dead because after he managed to steady himself, he drew a gun from his overall pocket. He told her to get off his property and not ever come back. So, I know people can have passionate feelings about land."

Ben shook his head as if there was an annoying ring in his ear that wouldn't go away. He put his opened hand over his face and squeezed his temples wondering why in the hell he had to deal with Rhoda at a time like that.

"Rhoda, you ever been out of War Gap before now?"

"Don't make fun of me, Ben. You don't know what I been through to talk like that to me." She bowed her head as if ashamed of her defensiveness.

"How about I don't make fun of you and you don't try to tell me things here aren't as bad as I think they are?" He looked at her until she finally looked up and held his gaze.

"I know," She said so quietly he had to read her lips, "Things are always just as bad as we think they are."

Rhoda slipped her finger back into the handle of the teacup and fidgeted with it absentmindedly. Ben regretted his words, feeling certain that whatever reason Rhoda had for wanting to die, it couldn't be enough to warrant his complicity in it.

5

Rhoda wasn't sure why she felt so calm. Was it the chamomile tea, the hormones from nursing Nanshe, or the distraction of Ben's stories?

She had been offered a bedroom upstairs with as much welcoming as Ben could muster. She understood now, after hearing his story, why he had been so upset with her. His situation was no different than hers, perhaps even worse because he had to hold it all in for Nanshe. And yet, maybe that made it easier. Rhoda would give anything to have someone to live for, an older child, or anyone able to ease her pain and make her feel necessary. Feeding Nanshe had given her just a glimpse of what it was like to have that, but it wasn't permanent or even real. Soon enough Nanshe would adjust.

Rhoda took off her shoes and placed them on the floor at the foot of the bed. She laid down on top of the quilt, not wanting to dirty anything, and used her coat as a blanket. The thick fabric was enough to fight the chill in the drafty room. As soon as her head landed on the pillow, exhaustion washed over her. If she could not yet die, the next best thing would be to sleep. She craved it so badly.

Her breathing slowed, but her mind still toyed with thoughts it refused to put away. She thought mostly about Ben's story of how he came to own his farm. It was a fascinating story which had her thinking a lot about Paumina. What kind of woman would marry an old man and care for him faithfully for ten years, only to then adopt an orphan to raise as her own? Had she never wanted to marry for love? She thought up possible scenarios as to why Paumina would not have wanted to get married, or why she never had despite a desire to do so. The possibilities were endless. Rhoda's mind loved to think about things with endless possibilities, but she wanted to ask Ben. She wanted to know, not just speculate. But she reminded herself she wasn't entitled to ask such personal questions.

Rhoda thought perhaps Ben would like to hear her own story of how she came to be at that place at that moment. But as soon as she thought it, she knew he probably would not. Still, she tried to imagine what she would tell him if he asked. Her story was nothing like his. None of her family were brave or generous. Her mother had been born as Sarah Cox and was raised in a Kentucky coal mining town near the Virginia border. At fifteen, she ran off to get away from her daddy whom, as she had said, wanted her to play mommy in the most evil of ways. Sarah was sixteen when she met Arthur Vickers while staying with cousins in Kyle's Ford, Tennessee. They had conceived Rhoda out of wedlock while making love behind Kyle's Ford Elementary school in October of 1937. Arthur had lit a cigarette afterward and dropped it while passing it to Sarah. It caused the grass to catch fire and within minutes the entire school had burned down. It's no wonder Arthur's family thought Sarah was no good. They weren't happy at all when she ended up pregnant and Arthur had to marry her.

Rhoda considered that maybe her own story was interesting in a sad kind of way. Maybe Ben would want to hear it, but it was still not very heroic. Her mother had never saved anybody, unless she counted the times her mother brought people to Jesus. Rhoda never bought into that religious stuff, the whole Holy Ghost nonsense. She had seen her mother take sadistic pleasure in Rhoda's punishments too often to consider her righteous. It had been quite easy for Sarah to get away with the act, pulling away Rhoda's favorite toys for no reason other than to make her cry. Sarah would lie and say Rhoda had done something wrong so that Grandma Vickers would be pleased with Sarah's 'use of the rod'. Grandma Vickers had loved to see Rhoda being punished and Sarah made sure to come up with a reason whenever she was around, which was often.

Grandma Vickers despised Rhoda, hated her enough to will her a pistol. Rhoda wondered if she had known just how often Rhoda had thought of shooting herself? Before having an actual gun, Rhoda had imagined a shadow of a gun, just an idea of a gun. When her head would fill with too much chatter, Rhoda would picture herself raising the shadow of a gun to her skull and blowing apart all the words. But after receiving

Grandma's gun, Rhoda no longer imagined the shadow. Instead, she imagined that exact antique pistol, holding it up to her head and pulling the trigger, shattering bone instead of thought.

Despite how violent it all seemed, thoughts of blowing up her brain had actually been comforting to Rhoda for most of her life. Perhaps Grandma Vickers had sensed that and only wanted to give Rhoda comfort by willing her a gun. Maybe Rhoda had her all wrong. Instead of wishing her granddaughter harm, perhaps she sensed the comfort Rhoda had felt in her secret imaginings. Maybe she was aware of the illusions Rhoda had of her own power to stop all the chaos in her head. All Rhoda had to do was imagine a bullet exploding the thoughts into silence and she would feel a spark of satisfaction not attainable any other way. She used to be afraid of giving in to thinking those thoughts; but she came to see it for what it was, a silencer. If anyone needed to silence their mind, it was Rhoda.

Even after drinking chamomile tea, nursing a sweet baby girl, and being distracted with the woes of someone else; she was still so worked up with thoughts she couldn't sleep. She tried to summon the exhausted feeling she had when she had first laid her head on her pillow, but it was long gone.

The minutes ticked by at a much slower pace than Rhoda realized. She was sure the sun would rise soon, but in fact she had only been in bed for an hour. She had thought about her bus rides and the man with a red and yellow umbrella. What kind of man carries a red and yellow umbrella? She thought of when she deboarded the bus and saw a boy holding a sign which said, BART BREWSTER. She wanted to wait on the bench at the bus station just to see what a Bart Brewster would look like. And last night, she remembered, a cemetery appeared like a manger under a star. Because most people fear graveyards, Rhoda felt safe enough to sleep by a large headstone. Cold, but safe, she had thought of Olivia, imagined her to be buried nearby instead of miles away. She wished, again, that Olivia had been cremated so she could have her child's body in possession. But then what would have happened to the ashes once Rhoda did it, killed herself? Maybe it's best the girl was buried with a headstone and family who may, or may not, put flowers there. What kind of flowers would Olivia have liked? Wild roses or perhaps common daisies? There were daisies by the roadside where Rhoda once walked home from school...

And around the thoughts went. Thoughts, circling through time and space, skimming across the ocean of worry Rhoda held inside herself. Thought after thought pricked her brain like needles pushed through her skull. She could not turn them off. She needed silence. She needed to sleep. But all she could do was think and think and think.

She set her mind to equations. She tried to account for every bit of money she had spent on her journey, not that money mattered to her at all, but because the absolute nature of numbers might help her go to sleep. She tried to focus on her addition so her mind would not veer off track. She didn't try to analyze why she had made each transaction. One item after another was added to the total as if all that existed was the item and the amount. No reasons. No right or wrong. No blame or shame. In the middle of trying to remember if she dropped one quarter or two into the beggar's cup, she finally fell asleep.

6

Rhoda woke up sometime before dawn. The half-moon shone a muted light through the window. For a moment, Rhoda couldn't figure out where she was. She rolled onto her back and felt the cold wetness of her sweater as it draped over her skin. Milk. Last night. Nanshe. Ben. The pistol. Olivia is gone.

She sat up instinctively. Her breasts were hard, painful, and full in their belief that Olivia was still alive. Rhoda stood and clutched her sweater, pulling it away from her chest so friction would not make her situation worse. She walked into the hallway half aware that she was looking for Nanshe. Rhoda didn't remember hearing her cry, but assumed a cry had triggered her milk to let down.

As she neared the stairs, she noticed the soft golden glow of a lamp in the living room. Her socked feet silenced her footsteps as she made her way down, slowly, listening. Ben was in a rocking chair with his back to her. He was gently pushing back with his legs, rocking with long, slow swings. She heard him speak and froze in place to make out what he was saying. Her heart pounded in fear that she would be caught spying.

"Oh, baby girl," Ben whispered his coo, "She will drink for her Pop. She will. Granny Mina says you are so fussy, but look at you drinking it all gone for Pop."

Rhoda smiled, happy for Ben and amazed by his gentleness. Her husband Ed would have never done such things. Watching them, Rhoda's joy was pushed aside with a crushing sense of loss as she realized Nanshe would not need her milk. She felt as though a dense cloud of suffocating smoke was growing up around her. It occurred to her that she would never feed an infant again. Her breasts, now expecting a child to latch and drink, were useless; her milk a waste.

She didn't know what to do. She didn't want to go back to bed. She wanted dry clothes but had none. She wanted to bathe, but had no right. She wanted to run away, but didn't want to be seen. She wanted to put a bullet in her brain, but had no gun. She wanted Olivia, but Olivia was dead.

Without knowing she had made a sound, a small gasp for air had escaped between her morbid thoughts. It caught Ben's ears and he jerked his head around to try to see her. But it wasn't until he stood up, a sleeping Nanshe in his arms, that he saw Rhoda on the stairs. Her eyes were wide with panic as tears wet her cheeks. She pulled at her wet sweater with both her hands to keep it away from her skin. She turned and ran back up the stairs.

Ben held Nanshe close with a large hand over her ear. He expected Rhoda to slam the door, but all he heard was a gentle click as it closed.

Ben carried Nanshe to the bassinet which he had set up beside his own bed. Nanshe had a room of her own, a yellow room. Its perfect primrose color had been chosen by Della. Nanshe used to sleep there and Della would rise in the night to feed her. But, with Della dead, Ben wanted Nanshe as close as possible. When he gently lowered her into the bassinet and placed her on her back, her little hands jerked back in alarm, but she did not wake. He stared at the jumbled blanket over her and vowed he would try harder to learn to wrap her as Della had, and as Rhoda had. He felt destined to fail as a mother and father both. Some things he knew he could never do as well as a mother, but he would try. He hoped that would be enough.

His heart went from warm to cold when he thought of having to go up and check on Rhoda. He knew from the look of her that her pain ran deep. He wasn't sure if he could carry anymore load.

He made his way to her door and gently knocked, waited for an answer, but none came. He did this again three more times before speaking quietly through the door's wooden panels. "If you need clothes, I can bring some. They're old, ain't fashionable in the least. But you're welcome to them if you need them. There's a bathtub in the downstairs bathroom where you can get cleaned up. Just tell me if you want the clothes and I'll put them by your door and leave you to your privacy."

He waited again until an internal buzzing in his ears replaced the silence. He began to get upset at her for not answering. Finally he heard her muffled voice say, "Yes, thank you."

Ben could not bring himself to give her anything of Della's. He went to the closet where Paumina had kept spare dresses over the years in case a worker might need one. Some had belonged to Paumina herself, but were deemed too out of style to be taken into town when she had moved. Ben glanced over the options, thought about Rhoda's size and determined the green 1940s shirtwaist dress would have a flexible fit. It reminded him a waitress's dress, but it wasn't terribly old looking. He imagined her walking into a train station and buying a ticket in that dress. He decided she would not stand out in a bad way. He wanted to make it easy for her to leave town.

He walked back and laid the folded dress by the door before knocking again, "It's here. I'm going out. I need to let the sheep out to graze. I'll be back soon, but if you need me, call from the back porch. I'll hear you."

He waited, but heard only silence. He assumed she had heard him so he walked away.

Rhoda had been unable to pull herself together enough to answer. She thought, if she were to open her mouth, she would surely cry out so loudly she would wake Nanshe. Her mind relentlessly spun with sharp spikes of memories raking the inside of her skull. The pain her mind was inflicting on her was ruthless and nearly unbearable.

She maintained her quiet so rigidly that she could hear the squeaking of the spring on the back porch screen door. Ben was gone.

Rhoda opened the bedroom door, retrieved the dress at her feet, and quickly (almost running) went to the bathroom at the end of the downstairs hall. She quietly shut the door behind her, locked it, and leaned against it to catch her breath. She felt as though she had locked herself away from herself. But she knew that was ridiculous because she could plainly see herself looking back from the bathroom mirror.

It was the first glimpse of herself she had allowed herself to take since getting off the last bus 35 hours before. She looked terrible. Her dark brown hair was in knots of matted clumps gathered at her neck. Her dove gray sweater was not only wet, but beginning to stain as her milk mixed with all the dust from her travels. She remembered the times along her journey when, in moments of anguish, she had dropped to her knees, crawled, lied on her side to cry, rolled to stare up at the sun, and even yanked at her yet-to-be-matted locks of hair. She recalled these acts now, staring at her filthy appearance, with a sentimental longing. She preferred destroying herself with abandon as opposed to staring at the effects of her destruction.

"What must Ben think of me?" She thought, then, "How could Paumina have believed I was offering charity when I look so in need of charity myself?"

Rhoda imagined Paumina in church later that day, imagined her telling the women's circle about her. Would Paumina say a homeless woman showed up at the door and she had helped the woman by encouraging her to help Nanshe? Maybe Nanshe hadn't truly been unwilling to drink from a bottle. Maybe Paumina tricked Rhoda to thinking she was of use when in fact Rhoda had never been needed at all.

This was what Rhoda's mind did to things. It warped the goodness, or erased it altogether.

She stepped closer to the mirror but she saw herself no more clearly than from across the room. If anything, being so close to the reflection of her own eyes made her think of her mother staring back at her. Their eyes were the same shape and dark coffee brown color. Sarah would have been so ashamed of Rhoda. She probably already was, believing Rhoda was starting a new life without her. No matter what Rhoda had chosen to do with life or death, Sarah had never approved.

Rhoda's disgust with her own appearance was overshadowed by the shame she felt at imagining her mother seeing her that way. Of course, Sarah had not actually seen Rhoda. But, that fact held no sway over Rhoda's self-hatred. She pulled the mirror to open the medicine cabinet and immediately took note of a thin pair of silver scissors. She took them, and without closing the mirror to look at herself, she began to cut her hair just above the matted clumps.

Handfuls of hair fell free into her grasp. Not wanting to make a mess of Ben's bathroom, she carefully placed one handful of hair after another into the trashcan by the toilet. The more she cut, the more calm she felt. When all the tangles had been snipped free, she set the scissors on the porcelain sink and ran her fingers through what was left of her hair. It felt choppy, long in places and short in others. When her fingertips reached the back of her neck where her skull connected to her spine, she felt a small nearly bald patch where the worst tangle had been.

Rhoda's calm began to be devoured by a sickness in her stomach. What she had done was crazy. What she had done was not normal at all. She hadn't needed to cut her hair that way, so why had she? She could have used an oil to break the tangles loose. She could have trimmed it nicely if she had looked in the mirror. What would her mother think now? What would Ben think? Rhoda couldn't let him see her. She needed to leave, find a place far away where no one who knew her would find her body.

7

Rhoda left the bathroom without looking at herself in the mirror. She was still not bathed, nor had she bothered to put on the clean dress. She walked out of the bathroom and entered what she assumed was Ben's bedroom, the room he had shared with his wife only a few days before. Nanshe lay sleeping in her bassinet. Rhoda avoided looking at her, afraid Nanshe would be awake and frightened by her monstrous appearance.

She only wanted to find the gun and go. She knew where men in Tennessee usually kept their guns, so she began her search by checking for a false wall in the back of Ben's closet. The wall their seemed solid. She then bent down to peek under his bed and saw only a glossy wood floor without even the tiniest bit of dust. The dirtiest thing in the room was Rhoda.

She stood and put her hands on her hips, twisting to look around the room. She tried to imagine she was Ben, mourning his wife after she had been murdered. She realized he had not told her how it happened. Had she been at home? Did they kidnap her first? She glanced around as her mind split, half thinking about finding a gun and the other half thinking about how murder happens. A vision popped into her mind of a pimply kid with blond hair and a rifle. His eyes were bloodshot as he coldly stared back at Rhoda. She gasped and stepped back, shaking her head until the image vanished from her mind.

"If I were Ben…" she whispered, then leapt onto the bed and moved her hands wildly about until one of them found its way under a pillow. There, her fingers touched the wood of the forestock and quickly wrapped around it, barrel and all. She yanked the shotgun from its hiding place and ran from the room with it clutched in her hand.

She ran up to the bedroom where she had slept the night before. In under a single minute she had slipped her shoes onto her feet, her coat onto her back, and made her way out to the front porch. She had carefully opened and closed the screen door with great effort not to make a sound. She had only two thoughts, don't wake Nanshe and don't get caught.

Once the door was closed, she stood and looked around the property. Ben had said he was going to feed sheep, but there was no sign of sheep anywhere ahead of her. The land before her rose in elevation so slightly, Rhoda would have labeled it flat. But she was used to mountains along every horizon. She remembered the pumpkin patch was in the direction up the sloping landscape and wanted to make sure she didn't get caught there twice. A number of trees were clustered together off in the distance to the left. If she ran quickly, maybe she could get there before Ben saw her.

She thought, "You are stealing his gun." But, she pushed the thought away. No one could arrest a dead woman.

She intended to take a deep breath and then run, but the breath was not completely inhaled before her legs took off toward the trees. She ran as hard as her legs would carry her, the gun clutched by its forestock in her right hand. She realized too late that she had forgotten to check to see if it was loaded.

Of course it's loaded, she thought to herself. Ben wouldn't have slept with an unloaded gun.

She had only ran a short way before her lungs began to burn from the effort. She told herself to desire the burn, to love the physical pain because it would override the pain twisting in her heart. Her mind echoed the words, "Burn, burn, burn, burn," as she forced her leg muscles to carry her. She needed air. She needed to breathe. Oh, God, she needed to stop running, but she wouldn't stop, not even when the ringing in her ears from her blood pressure rising off the charts began to sound like a fighter jet. She kept running.

It was the whirring and the ringing that prevented her from hearing Ben's footsteps running up behind her. He had been on his way back to the house when he saw her take off through the field, his rifle in her hand. She lumbered in her effort more than a girl her size should. Ben thought, again, that whatever she had been doing with her life had not been good for her. She was weak and pale, even for a White girl. He thought she might very

45

well keel over and die of a heart attack. But he would be damned if she was going to do it with his rifle in her hand.

He leapt the final distance between them and knocked her to the ground. He held her, face down, her arms flat to the ground under his large hands. The last thing he wanted was to be shot with his own gun. "What are you doing?" He demanded to know, "And what the hell happened to your hair? Have you lost what was left of your damned mind?"

Rhoda just sobbed, the grass from the field got into her open mouth and became covered with drool as she cried and pleaded, "Let me go!"

"Hell, naw! You got my gun! What do you think they'll do finding a dead White woman with my gun? Do you not have a single thought in your head for anyone 'sides yourself?"

Ben yanked the gun free from her hand and moved off her. He sat cross legged and focused on his gun. He pulled back the bolt and opened up the chamber to remove the shot he had loaded there three days before. He was already sliding the ammo into his jacket pocket when Rhoda finally decided to stop crying into the grass. She sat up and faced him.

"I'm not selfish!" She screamed at him. "You are selfish! You took my gun from me because you're worried about you! You don't care if I live or die, so let me die!"

"I told you, die somewhere else. Maybe I should have also clarified that you shouldn't die with my gun."

"Just give me back my gun and I'll go." Rhoda wiped her eyes.

"Go where? Back up to the pumpkin vines? I don't

trust you," He finally took his eyes off his rifle and looked into hers. She was wild looking, almost scary with her hair all chopped off and her clothes a mess. The sympathetic feeling rising in him only made him uneasy so he forced more anger out at her to combat it. She didn't deserve his sympathy. "Didn't I tell you what's going on here? I buried my wife the day your ass showed up here. She was killed for no other reason than because we are Black and we dare have something a White man wants, that's all. We've fought like hell for decades to not die for living here, and yet you think I'm going to sympathize with you 'cause you want to die and I won't let you?" Ben rolled his eyes. "I think that sounds like the very definition of selfish."

Rhoda held his gaze like she had entered a staring contest, "The only thing that gives me peace is knowing that soon I'll be in the silence of death. It's all I have to hope for!"

"I hope it for you, too," Ben felt the words bite at his heart because he knew he didn't mean them. But the pent up emotions inside him were breaking loose beyond his control. He looked up to the sky and laughed with tears running from his eyes, "They want our land. They want our life. And now they're even jealous of our death." He looked back at Rhoda, his tears catching her off guard. He said, "And the truth is, I don't even want it. I don't want none of this no more. I'm so tired of fighting. But I have a daughter to think about."

"Yes," Rhoda said steely, "You have a daughter and you will watch her grow into a woman, get married, give you grandchildren. She has her whole life ahead of her and you get to share it with her. And even though your wife is dead, you love her still. You loved her for real. My husband never loved me, and now my baby can't either."

"My daughter," Ben's tears continued to flow but he felt no need to feel ashamed when staring into the face of a woman as messed up as Rhoda, "She might grow up if they don't kill her. How will I keep her safe here? She is a blessing and a burden. Maybe I'll see it differently when the wound's not so fresh. But right now, I don't know how to get out of this mess. Goddamn racists."

For a moment, Rhoda's mind ticked away trying to come up with solutions for Ben. Her brain never passed up an opportunity to fly off into what if. But part of her knew if she got too caught up in his problems, she'd back out of what she needed to do for herself. She had planned to die, not to live and solve problems. Every time she failed to kill herself, it became even more difficult for her to figure out how to be alive. She reached a hand up to touch the stubble at the back of her head. The option of staying alive continued to be more and more difficult to consider.

"I know you don't have it in you to care," said Ben, causing a stabbing feeling in Rhoda's heart, "But let's make a plan and you promise to stick to it. You stay inside the house, out of sight, until Paumina comes tomorrow morning, six a.m.. She can drive you out of here. I can't promise she'll take you where you want to go, but wherever it ends up being, I'll make sure you have your gun."

8

Ben ran the bath. Rhoda hadn't spoken or made a motion to indicate she was aware of her surroundings since they'd left the field. He only assumed she actually agreed to his proposal to wait for Paumina because she had not disagreed. Now she sat on the kitchen chair he had dragged into the bathroom. Her hands were together in her lap, her feet together on the floor, her back straight like she was in a classroom.

He placed his hand in the nearly full tub of water to make sure it was hot, but not scalding hot, and then turned off the faucet. In the absence of the sound of rushing water, he heard Nanshe's groggy cry. She was awake, but barely so.

"It's ready," he said to Rhoda who looked slowly up

at him as if she had so much to say but no longer a voice with which to say it.

Ben just shook his head at her and left the room. He felt annoyed, worried, angry, frustrated, and had no idea what the solution would be. He picked up Nanshe and carried her into the kitchen. With one hand he prepared her bottle while she was cradled in the crook of his other arm. Her head turned, her mouth moving over the fabric of his sleeve in search of a nipple. It was her instinct, he knew, but he wondered if Nanshe remembered Della at all. Did Nanshe recall, or had she ever been aware of the joyful tears in Della's eyes almost every time she watched Nanshe nursing?

Della had been such a strong woman, built solid from her wide feet to the top of her head which contained a quick witted mind and stubborn ideas. Della had not been afraid of trouble, whether it was a simple physical challenge or something more complicated. Ben had often marveled at his wife and wondered why she had stuck around. Sure, he had no financial problems and he was a hard working man. But she was fully aware of the rumors about his land being cursed. She had said she didn't believe it and knew all the trouble stemmed from the racist people of Grand Saline, not a deity or devil. And that made him admire her even more. She knew the risks were real, not fairytale, yet she took him on anyway. She married him. She loved him. She gave him a family the likes of which his old farmhouse had never seen.

By the time Ben had the bottle heated, he had to wipe his eyes with the sleeve of his flannel shirt. It was only a matter of time before the permanence of Della's death truly sank in and he'd have to mourn her completely. He had planned to wait for Paumina to be gone, but then Rhoda came. If there ever was a thing to make him start to wonder if the curse was real, it would be the materialization of Rhoda. At first he thought she would stumble on out of there like a dog with her tail between her legs, possibly cause trouble if she reported her gun stolen. Once he had realized she wasn't about to leave without it, he expected her to, at minimum, comprehend the gravity of his situation. That hadn't happened either. Rhoda's mind seemed lost in a far away place. Ben wouldn't be surprised if two months out Rhoda wouldn't have any idea she'd even been to his house, that is, if she was alive that long.

Ben sat in the kitchen chair and placed the bottle to Nanshe's lips. She had caught on quickly that the bottle would be her new source of food and made no effort to reject it. Her eyes squinted in the light of the newly risen sun as she scanned the features of Ben's face. He had, obviously, never fed her while Della was alive. Not only did Nanshe need to figure out the strange, rubbery bottle nipple; she also had to figure out who was this big, scruffy new mother of hers. Ben smiled and let out a little laugh as he looked down at her. "Yesterday, you had that wrinkly old mother with the big hat, and then you had that white breast, oh my, that was different. And now this big scruffy looking man is being your mama. Will things ever be normal for you, Nanshe? Not in this house, sweet girl."

Nanshe listened, her eyes watching Ben's lips move with the words. Her tiny head and arms jerked a bit as if she felt an inexplicable need to respond but had no control over herself to do so. Ben watched her in amazement until she had consumed the last drop of formula and took a few slurps of air. He watched her suck in her bottom lip a couple of times and her eyelids droop heavily. He stood, propped her up against his chest with a firm hand on her back, and bounced gently on his toes and hummed until Nanshe let out a big burp followed by a slight hiccup. Ben laid her back into the crook of his arm and continued to bounce until her tiny arm went limp and fell to her side in sleep. Ben was again reminded that he needed to work on his swaddling skills.

After getting Nanshe back to her bassinet, his mind returned to Rhoda. He had had a nice reprieve from dealing with her. But now that she was back on his mind, he realized he had not heard any sounds from her to indicate she was bathing. Like a punch in the gut, he wondered if she had drowned herself... in his bathroom.

He ran to the bathroom and didn't bother to knock before shoving open the door. He could see the back of Rhoda's head, the hair a mess, and her arms draped over the edge of the tub. She was not submerged under water, which was good. But she did not seem the least bit startled or responsive, which was bad. He stepped closer, could see her knees, and closer, so that all but her face was visible to him. She was so still that the water was calm and clear of ripples like glass.

Rhoda had looked so much older to Ben when he had first seen her than she did now. Her stomach appeared soft and fleshy. Her thighs and hips donned stretch marks, pink with newness. He thought of the feel of Della's stomach before and after she had given birth to Nanshe. Ben was overcome with unexpected longing for his wife. Why was this woman here and Della not? Rhoda would have willingly taken Della's place. It all seemed so unfair.

Ben thought, if only he were alone, he would finally

let loose the pain he held inside. But he wasn't alone. He forced himself to stop thinking about it. He had already proven he could rein in his emotions for the sake of Paumina, and now he needed to do it for his pride in not wanting to seem like a fool in front of a stranger. He was afraid of the moment he would be alone and have to let himself feel all the pain welling up inside of him. He was afraid because what had built up within him was thick and heavy like a dark and whirling Texas sky just before a tornado.

He needed to hold it together, for at least the rest of the day.

"Your head's a mess," he said.

"Yes," Rhoda breathed out the word, but didn't move. "It won't stop thinking. All the time. Do you have injections to tranquilize sheep? Stab my brain with one, please."

Ben almost laughed, "Sheep are already pretty tranquil. And I meant your hair was a mess."

She moved a hand up and around her head, haphazardly feeling the choppy job she did. "God," she sighed.

"Let me give it a try, see what I can do to fix it. You couldn't look any worse."

She didn't respond. He walked past her to the medicine cabinet and retrieved the scissors. Then he grabbed the kitchen chair he had brought in earlier and carried it over to sit behind her head.

He was used to shearing sheep, had memorized the necessary motions so that he did it without consciously thinking about the sheep as having feelings. Because of that, he tilted Rhoda's head from side to side with a bit more force than others might have. Bend, snip, comb, tilt, cut, comb. He preferred to think of her head as just a head, not attached to a suicidal, grieving, backwoods White girl.

He pushed her head forward, "Damn. That there is going to have to grow out. No blending to it unless I shave your whole scalp. Why'd you do this to yourself, anyway?"

Rhoda didn't answer. She had a little less than 24 hours to keep herself together until she got her gun back. Now that she had a time frame, it was as if her body just shut down from exhaustion. She didn't want to speak or hear. She didn't want to move, not even when the water in the tub was freezing cold.

Ben pulled the comb through her hair and she could tell it was short. She assumed she probably looked like a man. That thought made her mind start ticking.

"Would you have treated me the same way if I were a man? Taken my gun from me? Or would you have let me shoot myself?" She laid her head back against the edge of the porcelain tub and looked up at him.

He held the scissors in one hand, opened as if he was about to snip something, and the comb in the other. He looked surprised at the sight of her upturned face, as if he had forgotten she was in the room.

"I'd have shot your ass on sight. Now, a week ago? I'd have asked what you needed. Yesterday? Boom." He moved his hands out like an explosion. "It's probably best for me that you aren't a man. I'd be in jail and Nanshe would be raised by a woman likely to die before she graduated high school."

"Don't underestimate how a woman can stay alive just 'cause she's needed," Rhoda sat up in the bath and pulled her knees up to hug them. She was trying to prepare herself for the chill of getting out of the water.

"What the hell is that?" Ben said when he saw her back. Small round scars dotted up and down her spine like a hundred injection sites, only bigger than a needle. His mind conjured all kinds of sheep farming analogies in a failed attempt to figure out what might cause such marks.

"You know what they are," Rhoda sighed and stood up, water splashing and dripping off her. She barely gave the water time to fall before she stepped out onto the green rug.

"No I don't," Ben said defensively as he eyed similar marks, stretched out by the gained weight on her bottom. "How would I know such a thing?"

Rhoda didn't answer. She took a mint green towel from the towel bar and dried herself off. Ben watched her with a mixture of the usual man-staring-at-naked-woman attention and the way he would have looked at an injured animal. She slid the green shirtwaist dress on over her head and buttoned it up carefully, trying to keep it from touching her painful, naked breasts. After her fingers twisted the last button through its slot, she walked out of the room, leaving her dirty laundry in a pile by the tub.

"Twenty-four hours." She said from somewhere in the hall.

9

Rhoda went back up to the bedroom where she had slept the night before. She intended to sleep away most of her last day; but she always managed to underestimate her brain's ability to ruin plans she made.

Lying on her back, keeping very still, she stared up at the ceiling and sighed. She was cold, but didn't want to get under the quilt. She was hungry, but hoped the pangs would distract her from more useless thoughts. She made every effort not to think about her breasts, which still hurt but were no longer leaking.

"We give up," she whispered to the swirling patterns on the ivory paper covering the ceiling.

She was up there in the bedroom less than an hour before Ben knocked on the door. He didn't wait for an answer, now expecting with good reason that he wouldn't get one.

"Come eat breakfast," he said. "Paumina don't allow anyone eating in their room unless they're sick and dying."

"I am dying," Rhoda pointed out.

"Not today, you aren't. Now come on." He turned and walked away, leaving the bedroom door open.

Rhoda didn't follow. She stayed in bed and listened to her stomach rumbling and rolling, feeling the twisting and tightening of her insides. Eating would ruin it.

Sometime within the next hour, Ben appeared again. He was holding a bowl in one hand and a blanket in the other.

"I thought Della was stubborn. Ain't no woman alive that compares to you in that department. Were you always this way or is this just 'cause you have decided to die tomorrow?" He set the bowl down on the nightstand. "It's cold oatmeal. You tell Paumina and I'll tie that pistol up on a pole out of your reach 'til Wednesday."

"You couldn't stand me being here that long."

"Right," Ben agreed and placed the folded blanket at her feet. "I have to admit you seem much more calm. Maybe you should try getting clean more often."

"I was clean when I left Tennessee," Rhoda felt herself getting defensive and it was setting her on edge again.

"Does anyone there know why you left?"

"No. Why? Are you trying to figure out who to call to come save me?"

"I thought you might want to write a letter, say what you need to say before you can't say anything ever again."

Rhoda tried to assess if he was playing tricks with her mind, pretending to accept that she was really going to kill herself. She considered that perhaps he believed she was faking for attention. The thought of that made her sick to her stomach. Thinking of her stomach made it growl loudly.

"I'm not feeding it to you," Ben sat on the bed by her knees.

"How did she die?" Rhoda asked. The question surprised even her. She had wanted Ben to stop talking about her past, but she was careless in how she changed the subject.

"I told you that." The playful spark in Ben's eyes faded. He should have known better than to toy with her. Trying to be nice to a White girl was dangerous in a lot of ways, not the least of which was the assumption that Black men owed them an explanation of their own business. Ben kept his mouth closed tight and refused to say more about it.

Rhoda sat up and crossed her legs. She picked up the bowl and took a bite of the oatmeal, cold but creamy and smooth. It would have been delicious an hour ago. "Did you see it happen?"

Ben shook his head and looked out the window. He wanted to walk out of the room, but for some reason he couldn't. He felt it coming, the moment when he'd have to look at the night Della died and accept every bit of its ugliness. He wasn't sure if he was ready.

"Then how do you know she was murdered?" Rhoda set the bowl back on the nightstand, deciding it would be rude to eat while discussing such a topic.

"We were in bed, just this Thursday night," Ben glanced at Rhoda, half hating her for making him talk

58

about it. He looked away from her and visualized the details of that event, Della in bed kissing his shoulder, his cheek, his lips. He decided not to mention all that to Rhoda. But his body ached at the thought of Della's body against his as if it had just happened that very morning. He remembered how it had felt so new after so long waiting for her to heal from having the baby. Della's body had been warm and inviting, no longer that of a young eager girl. She had felt to him like home multiplied by ten. They had taken their time. As he thought of her, Ben looked back out the window, focusing as far into the distance as he could see.

Rhoda's voice interrupted his thoughts, "How did it happen?"

He reacted to the pain of her question by closing his eyes tightly. He would have to look at the details of that event sometime. He decided he would do so now for his own sake. He needed to get the words out in the open. "Nanshe started to cry and Della went to feed her. I fell asleep while she was gone. When I woke and Della wasn't back, I assumed she was asleep in Nanshe's room. It wasn't until Nanshe began to cry at four in the morning that I realized Della wasn't there. I checked every room expecting to find her passed out asleep or something."

Ben forced his voice to stay steady. "Nanshe was screaming to be fed and I couldn't think straight. I was screaming Della's name, mad at her, worried, confused. I ran outside with a flashlight, still screaming her name. The first place I checked was the barn. I found her there, naked, beaten, already dead. Her face was unrecognizable. I should have checked for her sooner..." His voice trailed off and his jaw clenched tight.

He stopped talking, but Rhoda's mind ticked away at

the what if and wouldn't leave it alone. She imagined Nanshe screaming all that time for her mother. She remembered the first time she had heard Nanshe cry and how it ripped her apart inside. How sad she felt to imagine Nanshe crying all that time.

"What did you do?" Rhoda asked, wondering if he had been able to soothe Nanshe.

"I fell on my knees and gathered her up in my arms and carried her back to bed," now the tears came. "I don't remember it all, my mind refused to process it," he breathed. "I just wanted to put it all back like it was before. I couldn't let her go, but she was already gone. She looked so bad…" Ben bent over and pressed his palms to his face and sobbed, gasping and trying to breathe. "I can't tell it all," he cried, loud enough that Rhoda worried Nanshe would wake. "I can't say it all out loud, oh god, but I know what he did to her. I saw her body and I know how she was violated. I want to grieve for her and I want to be angry but I can't do both at the same time or I'll kill the motherfucker. I'll goddamn blow his fucking head to pieces."

Rhoda moved behind him and wrapped her arms comfortingly around his neck. She leaned herself against his back like somehow her body would be enough of a shield to keep the pain away. She understood the loss he was feeling but at the same time it seemed foreign. No one in her family would have mourned a spouse that way. Ed certainly wouldn't have cared much if Rhoda had been murdered, no matter how violently.

Ben's body shook with sobs. "I should have warned her, told her about the sheep I'd found slaughtered. But I didn't want to scare her," he cried. "I was used to harassment. I should have taken it more seriously. I

60

should have never fallen asleep without her."

"You loved her so much, Ben. It's not your fault." With her arms crossed over his chest, she squeezed him tightly. She wanted to comfort him and it made her feel useful. But Ben was not even aware of Rhoda's presence. All his body felt was pain and loss. At that moment, a pack of dogs could have eaten him alive and all he would have thought about was Della.

He tried so hard to steady his voice and stop crying. His effort made his words come out sounding angry, "She should have never married me. I let her down."

"Don't think that way. Her last thoughts were probably worrying about letting you down, and you would never want her to feel that way. She wouldn't want it for you, either."

"You don't know her! Don't try to tell me her last thoughts!" Ben surprised Rhoda by pulling himself out of her arms and standing to face her. He tried to stare at her but could barely see her through the black shadows created by his rage. He looked in her direction, but saw only the Whiteness of her face. "Who do you think you are to come in here and try to replace her?"

"I wasn't…" Rhoda stammered, confused.

"You're a White woman aren't you? Yes, you're a trickster pretending you don't want anything, but there's something you want, isn't there? This is not coincidence or fate. You feed my child from your breast, you show yourself naked in front of me, you try to seduce me and trick me because you want them to arrest me or kill me. It's true isn't?" Ben felt like his feet were not even on the ground. He was in a fast moving river being pulled by a relentless current of annihilation. No matter how hard he resisted, he couldn't break free, so he gave into it. He leaned in close to Rhoda until she had to back away. His face was distorted by rage.

"This isn't who you are, Ben." Her words came out in a whisper.

"You don't know who I am, bitch! And you don't know my wife. You're nothing like her. You're just like the rest of them. You make me sick just to look at you."

Rhoda's heart was crashing down in a spiral; her chest muscles constricted tighter and tighter until she couldn't breathe. She had not even realized she had begun to hope until suddenly hope disappeared. She pleaded for some sign that what she feared was not really about to happen. "Think of Della--"

The pain of the slap across Rhoda's face shocked her into silence. Ben's words came to fill the void, muffled at first, then growing loud and more clear.

"Don't you say her name! You have no right to it!"

Ben's eyes seemed to look in the direction of her eyes, but were focused far away, straight through her, into some illusion she could not see. Rhoda remembered the day they had fished Olivia's body from the water. When Vaughn Crumbly carried the baby's bloated body up the front porch steps, Rhoda had run out screaming. Her fists slammed into Vaughn's chest and shoulders over and over until one of the rookie firemen pulled her off. It's a wonder Olivia's body hadn't been dropped in the chaos. Rhoda knew how Ben felt. She knew whatever he was about to do was part of mourning. She was terrified and tried her best to redirect him.

She said, "I know you are hurting and you miss her--"

Ben grabbed Rhoda up, grunting with anger, and threw her back down on her stomach. He shook with a failed attempt to control himself. His only clear thought was that he didn't want her to see him. His body fell on hers, the weight of it knocking the breath from her lungs as the bedsprings creaked. His hands wrapped around her neck and squeezed. He wanted to erase her, but at the same time was terrified he would kill her. He fought with himself not to hurt her, yet he wanted vengeance. His fingers pushed into the skin of her neck and he heard her gasping for air. He wondered if Della had gasped for air as blood had filled her lungs from being beaten to death.

Rhoda began to silently cry, not because she felt she was about to die, but because she knew he'd come out of his state of despair and hate himself for what he was about to do. She knew because most of her life was spent in a similar emotional turmoil. Time and time again, her lashing out had painted her into a corner she couldn't leave until she destroyed a piece of herself. Every episode was more magnificent and terrible until her only hope became a bullet for her brain. She didn't want that for Ben, but she couldn't have cared less about her own body. She hated it as much as he did.

Rhoda saw the late morning sunlight seeping through her closed eyelids. She focused on the redness and attempted to get lost in it, preparing herself to die without fighting. But suddenly Ben let go and sat up on his knees. His hands and fingers shook. He could barely see through the tears in his eyes or hear for his blood slushing like a flood near his eardrums. He wanted release from the pain and he wanted to avenge Della's death. But when he caught sight of Rhoda through blurry vision, he saw her dress had inadvertently been hoisted up exposing her nakedness. He again caught sight of the round scars on her spine and across her bottom.

He sat back on his feet. The world was suddenly still and quiet as if every part of it was shocked by his actions. Rhoda laid motionless except for her chest rising and falling with steady breathing. Ben ran his fingers up over her spine. He had not completely quelled the last of his rage and fought an urge to claw at Rhoda's skin until it ripped off her bones. But a curiosity about those marks seeded reason into the mind of the monster into which his grief had transformed him. All it took was two seconds of clarity to know those scars were from cigarette burns.

10

Ben fell onto Rhoda as if no longer able to hold himself upright. He wrapped his arms around her, making sure not to touch her breasts, and wept into what was left of her hair. He said nothing at all, no apology, no explanation for what he had done and almost done. There was no apparent realization that the weight of him made it hard for Rhoda to breathe. He just cried.

Rhoda felt relieved that he had reined in his anger on his own. She also felt guilty. She thought, if she had stayed in Tennessee, what would Ben be doing now? She imagined he would likely have hurt himself in some way because he obviously felt partly to blame for Della's death. But the guilt of hurting a self is much easier reconciled than the guilt of hurting another.

Finally, Rhoda had to move to get air. In response to the feel of her pulling away, Ben rolled off her and onto his back. His hands covered his face as he continued to cry. Rhoda sat up and pulled her dress collar away from her neck where bruises were sure to arise. She watched as his body shook, his chest heaved to pull and push air from his lungs; his mouth was open and his face was wet. Days of pent-up pain flooded from him, freeing him while it slashed and ripped at his heart.

Rhoda considered staying quiet and saying nothing as she recalled how Ben had responded to the last few things she'd tried to say. But what she wanted to say felt right, so she had to say it. "You can't blame yourself for what other people have done."

"I don't know why I did that," Ben said.

"Because mourning makes us sick," Rhoda offered the excuse.

"Oh, god! Am I going to end up like you?" Ben's stomach showed visible signs of tightening at the nausea he felt just at the thought of it.

Rhoda let out a laugh, but worried Ben would take that as further proof of her craziness. "Impossible. You would have had to be born this way."

Ben wiped his face with his shirttails, and finally looked at Rhoda. "I'm sorry. I don't know what I'm doing."

"You're being hurt and angry," Rhoda looked away, feeling a sense of awkwardness growing between them. "How could anyone know how to navigate this?"

"But you aren't to blame for what happened here." Ben put his hand over hers.

"No. But, I'm an easy target. It's okay."

"Is that what you told whoever burned your back?"

Ben moved his hand to put a finger on her spine, then promptly stopped touching her.

"Mama did that."

"When you were little?"

Rhoda nodded and stared at the wall where a framed print of roses in a vase hung slightly off-center.

Ben asked, "Is that why you're so fucked up?"

Rhoda shrugged. "It hurt, but it brought the silence. It meant she was finished berating me and my mind was numbed by the pain."

"What about your husband?" Ben asked.

Rhoda smiled at Ben's newfound calm but tried to hide her expression from Ben. His outburst seemed to have served the same purpose within him as her suicidal thoughts served within her. His voice was steady and he was asking about her life, which meant his own demons were temporarily silenced. She answered, "He wasn't abusive, if that's what you're asking. He was too cowardly. I had confused his cowardice as strong morals and selflessness. Even though he never beat me, his cowardice was destructive."

Ben didn't respond so Rhoda continued, wanting to keep Ben's mind on her problems instead of his own. "Our baby was born with Sturge-Weber Syndrome. The top half of Olivia's face was covered with a purple splotchy birthmark like a spotted mask. She would have likely had learning problems, but she was too young for us to know the extent of those. Mama said my sins caused it. Ed couldn't stand the thought of people thinking badly of us. He forbid me from leaving the house with Olivia and refused to let anyone but Mama visit. Ed couldn't even bring himself to look at Olivia. When Mama called and said she wanted me to go with her to the church to help clean the sanctuary, Ed told me to go on and leave Olivia with him. I didn't want to leave her, but I told myself it might give Ed a chance to bond with her. But I couldn't shake the terrible feeling I had. I rushed. I've never cleaned so fast in my life. I worried he would neglect her if she cried. With the way he acted, I still don't know how he managed to get the courage to put his hands on her and carry her out to the Buick. He left me a note, explaining his reasons for driving off the bridge. But, truthfully, he was just a sorry excuse for a human being. You, Ben, are not even close to being like him. It's not your fault what happened to your wife."

"All I can see are the ways I could have prevented it."

"Me, too. That's how I've felt my whole life about almost everything, but never as much as I feel it about Olivia. It was always, how do I prevent the pain that's coming? Once it comes, it stays, builds up inside me. Every way I've tried to prevent it or erase it has only made it worse. But, eventually I won't have to try anymore."

"I'm sorry," Ben said again and sighed. "Losing Della is so hard to deal with and I've tried to be strong for everyone else. I haven't even started to process her not being in my life, or what lies ahead."

"You won't have time to worry about what comes next. Nanshe will see to it that you're too busy right here and now." Rhoda's heart ached at the thought of caring for a baby. She hadn't realized she was wincing.

"Did I hurt you?"

"Not like you think."

"I bet you think I'm a monster."

Rhoda knew Ben was nothing like Ed, and she didn't

even consider Ed to be a monster. "Obsessing over what other people think of you is self-destructive and only hurts the people you think you're helping."

"Like a monster."

"Just don't." Rhoda sighed, wondering if she was helping or making things worse. She got up and walked out of the room without explanation.

Downstairs in the bathroom, she used the toilet even though she didn't really need to. She just needed a reason to be away from Ben, end the conversation before he spiraled into self-hatred. Self-loathing was her job and she didn't think it suited Ben at all. She saw him as the loving father to Nanshe, loving husband to Della, and that was all she would allow herself to consider.

After flushing the toilet, she washed her hands at the sink and stared into the mirror. Her first thought was that she looked a lot like Bob Dylan. The little bit of natural curl in her hair had really sprung up due to whatever she and Ben together had done with it. But, that was just the top, which was spared the worst of her attack. The back of her hair was cut very short, like a Navy recruit. Rhoda thought she looked comical and understood why Ben had thrown her face down on the bed so he wouldn't have to look at her.

Her mother's voice came to mind, "They'll hurt you if you're pretty or ugly, Rhoda, but they'll only please you if you're pretty."

She looked at the shape of her long nose and her thick eyebrows, the way her mouth had a natural pout. She tightened her lips and gave herself a firm stare and nearly laughed aloud at how much she looked like a man. She wondered what her mother would say, and then shrugged at her reflection. It didn't matter. Perhaps

Paumina would give her a hat. She could comb her hair into bangs and that should be good enough to get her through the day with few suspicious stares.

But she still had half of the present day to get through. The big question in her mind was, should she try to comfort Ben or would he be better off if she stayed away from him? He seemed to be ambivalent about having her in his house. She decided she would go back into her room and stay, try to sleep as much as possible, and if Ben needed to talk he would find her.

Just before she walked out of the bathroom, Nanshe began to cry. Rhoda fought back the urge to go to her and stood motionless with her hand on the doorknob. Soon, she heard Ben's heavy footsteps on the stairs, down the hall, and then she heard Nanshe grunt and whimper to indicate she had been picked up but was still unhappy.

When Rhoda was certain Ben had Nanshe in the kitchen, she opened the bathroom door and made a quick dart for the stairs.

Ben called from the kitchen, "Rhoda, come here!"

She froze, contemplating running up the stairs and pretending she hadn't heard him. She figured he had something he thought he needed to say to her, but she wasn't sure if it was a good idea to continue their previous discussion. She decided she'd go to him and leave if she felt it was bad for her to be there.

"Yes?" She asked, stepping into the kitchen.

"I thought you might want to feed her, since you'll be leaving soon. It's okay if you don't want to, but I wanted to offer."

At first, the idea made Rhoda's stomach tighten and twist. She remembered the pain she had felt while feeding Nanshe the last time. But, judging from the bottle Ben was warming, he did not intend for her to breastfeed the baby. She also considered that Ben was trying to right his wrong, for his own peace of mind. For that reason, she went to the kitchen chair and sat.

"Okay," she said.

Ben carried Nanshe to Rhoda, gently lowering the squirming, grunting child into her arms.

"Look at her trying to hold up her head," said Rhoda, forgetting her apprehension. "How old is she?"

"Almost two months old." Ben squirted liquid from the bottle onto his wrist to check the temperature, then handed it to Rhoda.

"Olivia was five weeks old. Her little head was quite wobbly, but her big eyes would hold me in their gaze for long periods of time. I would study her and she would study me."

Nanshe's head jerked a bit to the side, overshooting the bottle's nipple and needed to turn back to latch on. Ben said, "She's got the hang of it now."

A silence settled on the room as they watched every move Nanshe made in awe. She was all that existed for the entire fifteen minutes it took her to consume the liquid and begin to slurp air. Rhoda pulled the bottle from Nanshe's lips and passed it to Ben. She wanted to kiss Nanshe's forehead and sing to her, but was mindful of Ben's accusation that she was trying to replace Della. She had no such intentions and had to be careful not to be misunderstood.

"Feeling better?" Ben had rinsed out the bottle in the sink and was just sitting back down in the kitchen chair.

"It's peaceful to feed a baby."

"Maybe you should have another one."

Rhoda shook her head, keeping her eyes on Nanshe.

"Why not? If it makes you happy… It has to be better than dying."

She looked up at him now. "There's no outrunning it."

"Dying? Hell, all you have to do is go someplace new and start over. You're White. You can live anywhere you want to live."

"My brain. That's what I can't outrun. It's always rambling on with painful ideas."

"Is it doing that right now?"

"No. But it will."

Ben shook his head. "I have to tell you, I can't stand the thought of it. I feel like I ought to be able to change your mind."

"Because you want to make amends?"

Ben looked away. "Things are messed up right now. God, I am so sorry." He looked back at Rhoda and she could see the pain in his eyes, "How'd I let myself get this low?"

"I hope you can get past this idea that you've caused all this. It's not your fault."

"What I did up there?" He pointed his thumb back over his shoulder toward the stairs. "No, I have to take responsibility for that. No one made me do that. It was the hate in my heart and I don't want any part of it. That was my wakeup call that I can't think no more about revenge. I have to find peace and you could help by accepting my apology instead of telling me don't apologize!" His voice grew loud and his pitch became high and anxious.

"I accept your apology," Rhoda said, but when his eyes landed on hers, she said it again, "I accept it. Now you accept mine for--"

"I'm glad you're here." Ben cut her off before she could make her own apology for being so intrusive and insensitive. "You've been a nightmare, but you've given me a lot to think about. I don't believe in God. But I can't help but feel like there's a divine hand in all this. Maybe I'm just crazy--"

"Aren't we all?"

11

Rhoda washed the breakfast dishes and examined the contents of the fridge. There wasn't much, enough milk for cereal, half a carton of orange juice, a part of a roll of country sausage, two eggs, and a jar of purple jam which looked like blackberry but Rhoda couldn't be sure without taking off the lid. She assumed there must be a cellar for canned items, or perhaps a freezer for meats. She would have asked Ben, but he had gone out to make a routine check on the sheep and the rest of his property. Rhoda wanted to cook dinner, but she couldn't cook what wasn't there.

Outside the kitchen door, she found the cellar leading underground. In Tennessee, it would have been built underneath the house, but Ben's was partially buried in the yard with a small mound of land up over it. It had an outside lock for which she didn't have a key, so planning supper was pointless until Ben came back.

She went in and spread a blanket in the center of the living room floor and laid Nanshe face down in the center of it. Rhoda placed toys and interesting objects around her to encourage Nanshe to raise her head up and look around. The baby's tiny legs kicked, stretching the pink fabric of her sleeper. She needed a bigger size.

Rhoda thought about Olivia, how she had never even made it to the size Nanshe was now. Nanshe would get to do a lot of things Olivia never would. But Rhoda found it wasn't so heartbreaking to think of Olivia while watching Nanshe. The pain was still there; Rhoda's heart still ached for her own child, but the sight of Nanshe soothed her.

Rhoda stretched out on the floor beside the baby and watched her little bobbing head try to hold steady to make eye contact. Rhoda raised her own knees up and patted a steady beat as she began to sing the old bluegrass song, Pig in a Pen. Rhoda thought of her Uncle Brad and his banjo, how much she loved to hear him play and sing, and how seldom her family had visited him. Rhoda sang with all the mountain twang her Uncle Brad had used. Nanshe's head bounced in its effort to watch Rhoda singing the lively song. On the last verse, Rhoda lifted Nanshe and let her down on top of her own stomach. She hugged Nanshe, stroked her back, and gently bounced with the music. "Bake them biscuits, baby. Bake 'em good n' brown. When you get them biscuits baked, we're Alabam-y bound!" Rhoda giggled and sat up to hold Nanshe in her arms and look down at her. Nanshe's eyes were lit up from the excitement of the movements and sounds. Her tiny hand reached up to Rhoda's face but failed to have enough control to touch it. Rhoda leaned down and kissed her tiny palm. "You're so beautiful, baby girl, and how lucky you are! Your daddy loves you more than any daddy ever loved their baby girl. And your Mama loved you and fed you good and made you so strong. Look at you raising up that head and shaking that little fist."

Nanshe shook her head a little, then grinned up at Rhoda who could not have known it was the first time Nanshe had smiled at anyone. Rhoda bent and kissed her nose, startling Nanshe a little at first, but then she smiled again.

When Rhoda finally looked up from Nanshe's mesmerizing face, she saw Ben standing in the kitchen doorway, a steely expression on his face. Rhoda couldn't read it, and that was just as well. Ben knew how he felt inside, but he didn't know how he should feel. His heart was ripping in two, half of him feeling like Rhoda had stolen something from him, and the other half melting over the joy his daughter was feeling. He told himself it was just time for Nanshe to learn to smile, and it wasn't Rhoda's fault that Della never got to see it. Or had Della seen it? Ben didn't know everything that had happened between Della and Nanshe. Perhaps Nanshe had smiled for everyone except him. This thought was much more acceptable and his heart settled back to a steady beat.

"How long have you been there? Hopefully not long enough to hear me sing that old song," Rhoda blushed.

"What I want to know is, are you planning to run off to Alabam-y with my baby?" Ben smiled at the exaggerated Appalachian accent he had used to mock her.

"You're not so fancy sounding, either, Ben. Lots of people from my area came to settle here in Texas, so it's not so different."

"Now she's so scholarly," Ben walked over to sit on the couch near them. He leaned down to scoop Nanshe from Rhoda's arms. "Sit with me, sweet girl. We're going to listen to Rhoda give us a history lesson."

"Don't make fun of me," Rhoda turned away with embarrassment.

"Come on," Ben laughed, "I'm glad to see you happy for a change. Try not to force yourself out of it."

He waited, but Rhoda said nothing. She was still happy, she was well aware of how rare it was to feel the way she did. But she also knew there would be an inevitable turn. There always was. And if she tried not to be so happy, just rein it in a little, maybe the turn wouldn't hurt so much when it came.

Wanting to change the subject, Ben said, "Are you wanting lunch? We're having a delicacy of jelly on buttered bread and I brought in a couple of apples. I'll put on soup beans for our dinner."

"I can make the sandwiches," Rhoda offered.

"This isn't your house," Ben was smiling at Nanshe, avoiding looking at Rhoda. She couldn't tell if he was again implying she was trying to take over Della's place.

"I know, but I don't want to be a burden."

"I liked it better when you were singing," Ben handed Nanshe back to her and got up to leave the room. Rhoda listened to the tinking of spoons in jars and rattle of ceramic plates on counter tops. It reminded her of her mother. Every Sunday after church, Sarah had cooked a meal for anyone who showed up. Sometimes, but not often, Grandma Vickers would come. When she did, she would always point out what was wrong with the way the meat was cooked, or scratch away at an imaginary spot on the silverware. When everyone was finished eating, Rhoda would clear the table and wash the dishes while Sarah tried to entertain Grandma Vickers, which usually ended with a disagreement and Grandma Vickers leaving in a huff. Afterward, Sarah would come straight to the kitchen and slam dishes as she inspected Rhoda's work. That led to Rhoda being sent to her room, without fail, every single time. Rhoda couldn't understand why Sarah kept inviting the old woman over if it always ended the same way. And she couldn't understand why, if Sarah didn't like how Grandma Vickers treated her, did she treat Rhoda the same way? Of course, it wasn't exactly the same way. Grandma Vickers never laid a hand on Sarah, but Sarah never hesitated to lay hands on Rhoda.

Rhoda was so lost in her memories that she hadn't noticed Nanshe falling asleep. She carried her to the bedroom and placed her in the bassinet. She wrapped her yellow blanket snuggly around her. When she got to the kitchen, two plates were already on the table.

"I usually go to the store on Friday and buy a roast for Sunday. It didn't happen this time." Ben sat down at his plate.

"I'm sorry," Rhoda didn't know what else to say.

"Sorry for what? Sorry you didn't lug in a roast instead of that girly gun of yours? Well, I'm sorry about that, too." Ben's toast crunched loudly as he bit into it.

"I can never tell if you are mad at me or teasing me."

"I'm always mad at you, but what's the point in it? You'll be out of here by morning, so it shouldn't matter what I feel."

Rhoda picked up her toast and smeared on some jam. Bits of blackberry proved right her earlier speculations. "Right," she mumbled before biting into the bread. "Did Paumina make this jam?"

"Della," Ben answered, not looking at Rhoda. "She grew up in Arkansas on a farm about as big as mine, only with a lot more family living on it. They grew blackberries, had apple trees, grape vines, and fields of strawberries. She worked all her life, that's about the only thing our childhoods had in common."

"How did you meet?" Rhoda glanced at him, but he was still staring hard at his glass of ice water, so she focused on her bread.

"Her brother came to work for me, trying to earn money to buy his own place. He disappeared, we assumed he found better work elsewhere, but now I can't be sure. Della came looking for him. She was the most beautiful woman I'd ever seen. I couldn't take my eyes off her," Ben sighed and shook his head. "I'll never stop loving her. Now that I know what it felt like to be loved by her, I don't think I'll ever be happy with anything else. The world doesn't even seem real anymore."

"Did they find who killed her?" Rhoda's face grew hot with embarrassment for once again asking a prying question.

"Who killed her was never lost to be found. I know who did it. The police chief knows who killed her. But he won't arrest his own kin."

"Well, that isn't right," Rhoda was surprised by how Ben's resignation affected her. "Can't you do something? Maybe go above their heads and petition the state?"

"What the hell is 'petition the state'? I don't know what world you come from, but here there's no way to get around Police Chief Bowlin. If he were an honest man, maybe. But, he didn't get to be police chief by being an honest, upstanding citizen. He got there by promoting the same bullshit every other White man in this town thinks and feels in their wicked souls."

"Ah, Ben, it can't be that bad! It just can't be." Rhoda wiped her mouth with a napkin. "People back home talk bad about the Blacks and I never thought it was right, but they're just talking. They wouldn't never condone murdering anybody."

"You aren't from around here," Ben looked her in the eyes this time, forcing her to register her own words coming back to her.

"Well, why do you stay? You could sell and leave."

"This is my home, Rhoda. This is where I was born. I own this land. I will not be run off from my own home by evil men. I have to believe in my right to be here."

"So, you believe God put you here?"

"Did I bring up God? No. I'm talking about history, sacrifice, investment in the future, generations of people deciding to stay put here and make this something special. This place isn't here to serve me. I'm here to serve this place and make sure it isn't destroyed."

Rhoda remembered how she had felt the first time she found herself in the yard looking at the old yellow house. It had seemed alive. She understood what Ben was saying and suddenly felt like the house was scrutinizing her. She shivered.

"Do you ever feel like this place is haunted?" She asked.

Ben laughed, "I want to say you've lost your mind, but I think we've already established that." He stood and walked over to place his dishes in the sink. He ran water over a smear of purple jam until it rinsed away down the drain. When he turned off the water, he asked, "So, you still set on dying?"

"I wasn't thinking about it at the moment. But, I will soon enough."

"So, maybe you should consider the reason you aren't thinking about it right now and try to have more of that in your life."

"Sure. I don't know why I didn't think of that," Rhoda stood and took her plate to the sink and placed it on top of Ben's. He turned on the faucet again and let the water beat against it longer than necessary.

He said, "We all have to do what we have to do, I guess."

12

Rhoda threw the laundry in the dryer and pushed the start button. It groaned as it began to spin, whirring louder than expected. She hoped she had not inadvertently woken Nanshe. What she could not hear for the rumbling of the dryer and rhythmic slapping of buttons against the metal within it, was the sound of a knock at the door. She settled into an old leather chair in the corner of the laundry room and opened up last Sunday's newspaper. She was still humming that old Stanley Brother's tune, bouncing one leg while it draped over the other to the beat of the song.

From the living room, Ben peeked out the window to see who was knocking before he answered it. On the porch stood Police Chief Bowlin, his uniform stretched over his protruding stomach. Ben could see his white undershirt through the gaps between the buttons. With him were two other officers, each holding a rifle and looking around in all directions as if any minute someone was going to ambush them.

Police Chief Bowlin had his hand poised to knock again when Ben opened the door.

"Mr. Whitmer, you are under arrest for the murder of your wife, Della Whitmer. You have the right to remain silent..." Police Chief Bowlin continued his mandatory listing of Ben's rights, but his voice had turned into an indecipherable drone of noise as the thoughts in Ben's head took precedence.

Ben had thought this might happen, that he would be blamed for killing his own wife. But time and again he had pushed those thoughts from his mind. Even at this moment, he struggled to accept the unfairness. Police Chief Bowlin brought him out of his daze when he finally asked, "Are you alone?"

"Yes," Ben replied with no indication he was lying. All he knew was that the question seemed off in a way that scared him. He attempted to telepathically plead for Nanshe not to cry and for Rhoda to stay away.

"Good," nodded the police chief.

"I did not kill my wife, chief," Ben knew it was pointless, but he needed to say it aloud.

"You can tell us all you want back at the station where we'll take a statement, tell us all about how her dead body ended up in your bed. You need to come with us now."

The two other guys held their rifles just a little more rigidly.

Ben forced his voice into a submissive tone, "May I

please use the restroom before we go? I had so much water with lunch, I don't know if I can hold it into town."

"Don't try running, boy. I got two men out back, too; so you'll never make it out alive if you try to run. I'll give you ten minutes. Any more and we come in after you and I guarantee you, you won't like it if we do." He turned his head to spit off the porch, but kept his eyes glued on Ben.

Police Chief Bowlin didn't close the door until Ben had turned the corner down the hall. Ben was concerned he would be followed, but didn't dare look back. He entered the laundry room and closed the door behind him. Rhoda looked up from the newspaper in time to see Ben's expression of horror, a finger pressed against his lips to signal her not to speak. He stepped over to the dryer and cut it off, then went to Rhoda. He grabbed her wrists and pulled her to stand in front of him. His voice came rushed, whispered through tight lips. "I'm being arrested. They're charging me with killing my wife." Tears were in his eyes. "They're on the porch to take me now. I should have known they'd do this."

"They can't!" Rhoda said, but Ben clamped a hand over her mouth before she could speak more.

"Now, listen!" He whispered, pushing her back against the wall where his hand stayed cupped over her mouth. Rhoda's eyes became wide with worry and fear. Ben didn't have time to bother discerning if she was afraid of him or afraid of what the police might do to him. "I told them I'm alone. I don't want them taking Nanshe. I'll call Paumina to come as soon as they give me a phone call. But I need you," his grip tightened on her face for emphasis, "I need you to stay here. Stay calm. Keep my daughter safe until Paumina gets here. Do not lose your goddamn mind. You stay happy. You sing that hillbilly song. You take care of my girl until Paumina comes. You don't let nobody see you. You don't open a door for anyone. You stay in, you stay quiet, you stay sane."

Ben removed his hand and stared into Rhoda's eyes. She was confused, and terrified, but she nodded her intention of doing what he had asked of her. He looked at her mess of hair and reflected on how close she had been to dying when he had found her. They were together in their proximity to death despite their different feelings about it. Ben knew the desire of the police, his neighbors, the town itself was to be rid of him. They believed his death would solve all their problems. He pictured himself strapped to an electric chair and then his mind froze.

"Will you be okay?" Rhoda whispered, bringing Ben back to the present.

"I don't know. But, Rhoda, you have to believe me. You can talk yourself out of this killing yourself thing. You don't have to keep trying to die. I don't know if I'll ever see you again, because I don't know how I'll fight these charges if they say I did it, even though I swear I didn't. And I don't know if I'll see you again because you might blow your brains out as soon as I leave and you find your gun under my mattress." He noted the widening of her eyes. "I'm telling you where it is because I'm not a thief, Rhoda; I'm not a criminal. I'm trusting you to hold yourself together, not just for Nanshe…"

Ben leaned against Rhoda and pressed his lips to hers. It was a desperate kiss. Rhoda was surprised at first, but gave into the urgency of it even though she knew it wasn't really for her. It lasted only a minute, but felt like ten. When he pulled away, Rhoda saw he was crying.

"Why did you do that?" Rhoda whispered, biting her bottom lip nervously to keep it from quivering.

"Because I need you with me on this." He glanced from one of her eyes to the other, looking for evidence that she understood.

"I'm not going to let her get hurt, whether you kiss me or not."

Ben nodded, believing her. He didn't bother explaining further about the kiss. He wasn't entirely sure why he had done it. The urge followed a feeling of certain death which had risen up as he pleaded for her to take care of his child. He knew he may never see Rhoda again, never see Nanshe again, and never see Paumina unless it was through prison bars. He just wanted the last memory he had with the outside world to be one of love. And though he did not really love Rhoda in the way that's usually required before two people share a kiss, he did feel compassion for her. He reasoned that perhaps the kiss would distract her from isolating herself with thoughts of suicide. But that seemed to be a joke so poorly thought out that even he could not find humor in it. What Rhoda needed to survive could only come from within Rhoda.

"You don't deserve this," Rhoda stared into his eyes, looking for answers. "Surely justice is going to be served--"

"You don't believe that," he cut her off, "You know the world is unfair." He stopped short of going off into a tirade about injustice. He was trying to keep her from spiraling into depression. "All you need to worry about right now is you and Nanshe. And I want you to know I'm sorry if I hurt you."

Rhoda hugged him, understanding how it feels to want to be perfect and good to a world which seems flawed and mercilessly hurtful. To Ben, she had represented the world. She understood. And now, Ben was conflicted with that thought. Rhoda had no right to try to prove him wrong because she saw the world as being just as flawed and hurtful as he did. But it was different hearing such disdain from someone else. Others might believe the right thing for Rhoda to do was to talk him out of his darkness, but she knew that never would have worked on her. Still, she couldn't stand seeing Ben look so hopeless.

"I'll do everything I can," she whispered into his chest where her face was pressed.

"Just stay alive," Ben swallowed and began to pull free, but she held tighter.

"Thank you." She didn't say that she was thanking him for keeping her alive. She didn't say that she was thanking him for giving her a reason to want to live, even if only for a few hours. She didn't say that she was thanking him for trusting her, and for the kiss which still burned in her mind like the first warm day of spring. There was no legitimate reason for it, she knew. But the chemicals of the brain were so easily altered by hope, it cared little if it was hope of death or hope of love, nor did it care if it was logical or advantageous.

She kissed him again and filled up on the misguided sensations running through her body. What a fool you are, she thought of her brain, always making things more than they're meant to be.

13

Ben had told her to stay hidden, but she couldn't help but peek out the window as two police cars drove away down the long dirt driveway. Inside the first car, Ben was seated, handcuffed. His body rocked with the jostling of the car as it hit ruts and bumps. Even after the cars had disappeared from Rhoda's sight, she still felt like she wasn't alone, as if she were being watched. Perhaps it was Ben's warning haunting her mind, or maybe it was the house itself.

She walked over to the dryer to start it again, but reconsidered. Instead, she removed the clothes one at a time, shook them free of wrinkles, and hung them on a string that had been stretched across the far wall of the room. Ben's jeans, his white button-up shirt, Rhoda's jeans, her sweater, and three tiny sleepers were all draped from one end of the cord to the other. She was just doubling up on the clips to fasten a few pairs of underwear when Nanshe began to cry.

Instead of picking up the baby, Rhoda rolled the bassinet into the kitchen. She jostled it slightly along the way to distract Nanshe from crying. In the kitchen, Rhoda gently rocked the bassinet with her foot while she measured out formula for the bottle. The small amount of powdered formula left in the canister was worrisome. Rhoda estimated she could make no more than four bottles, which should last about eight hours. She hoped Ben would tell Paumina to bring formula; or in the mysterious ways of grandmothers, Paumina would just know it was needed.

Rhoda lifted Nanshe from the bassinet and cradled her with one arm while the other held the bottle. While feeding Nanshe, she walked to Ben's room where a telephone set on the nightstand. She stared at it, listening to Nanshe slurping happily, and considered calling Paumina herself. There was probably a reason Ben had not suggested it. Maybe he was worried the operator who would connect the call would report it to the police. It all seemed a bit overkill and paranoid, but wasn't that to be expected after Ben's wife had been murdered over a land dispute-- a race dispute?

She glanced at a notepad beside the telephone and saw a list of emergency numbers. The fire department, the police department, Central Christian Church - office, etc. Paumina's number was added in blue ink at the bottom in different handwriting. It was penned beautifully with long loops and perfect curves. Rhoda assumed Della must have written it. The pleasantness of the writing worked to soften Rhoda to the idea of calling Paumina herself.

Before giving it anymore thought, Rhoda picked up the telephone receiver and placed it to her ear expecting to hear the faint buzzing signal. She heard silence. The line was dead. She held the phone receiver out in front of her face and stared at it with puzzlement. Her first thought was that Ben had forgotten to pay his telephone bill. But, then she recalled the urgency with which he pleaded with her to stay hidden from view and how passionately he seemed to believe they were in danger. A shiver ran through her as she placed the receiver down harder than she had intended.

Nanshe's head bobbed with the motion of Rhoda's arm slamming the receiver in place. She grunted when she lost hold of the bottle. Rhoda held her close and managed to get her latched on again. When Nanshe finished the last few slurps, she began to suck air. Her face puckered in disappointment and she began to cry again. One bottle was not enough.

"Hurry, Paumina!" Rhoda said to the ceiling as if in prayer to God, but in her mind she imagined only the bright eyes of an elderly Black woman.

****

Paumina received the call from Ben around two o'clock, only a couple of hours after Ben had been locked up. She acted surprised to hear that Ben had been arrested, but she had suspected it would be only a matter of time. He sounded calm, too calm, the way he acted when he didn't want her to worry.

She had always sheltered her Benoni, kept him close to the farm and busy with work. Paumina felt responsible for Ben's inability to come to terms with the burden of racism. He had learned soon enough after becoming an adult just how terrible some Whites were. Her sheltering had caused the reality of it to be a shock to him.

Unlike generations past, Ben didn't want the farm to be known as a sanctuary for the victims of racism. He had wanted to run it just like any other fair paying farm. He wanted to sell wool and produce just like any other farm, and be respected for what he produced and no more. He had tried to demonstrate why he should be treated equally by his neighbors and the marketplace, and had expected they would do so, reluctantly or not.

Paumina had once thought perhaps times had changed and Ben would be able to influence the people of Grand Saline to see his goodness, his kind heart, and his equality as a man. His strong determination and respect for justice had reminded her of herself years ago and she wanted to believe in hope again. But her fears were confirmed as she spoke to Ben on the phone; her hope seemed foolish.

On the call, Ben urged Paumina to get Nanshe to a safe place. He made it sound as though she already had Nanshe with her, which was strange. Paumina assured him she would do as he asked. But after hanging up the phone, she began to question what a safe place would look like. What would Nanshe's life be like without her father? Paumina felt certain Ben would not be given a fair trial. He had seemed resigned to the fact he would be found guilty and spend the rest of his life in jail as an innocent man wrongly accused. Maybe he would even lose hope and confess to it.

Paumina was not inclined to give up. It was her turn, again, to be the girl she once was. She needed to fight for

Ben. She needed to get a lawyer, and not just any lawyer. She needed to speak with Vencher Thames, a Black lawyer out of Dallas. If she was to have any hope of persuading him to take a case in Grand Saline, she needed to see him in person and quickly.

She told herself Nanshe would be safe with Rhoda until she returned. Rhoda had seemed troubled, but Paumina had seen many troubled people in her days. Big hearts that felt every slap the world had to offer often ended up caged inside a troubled soul. Rhoda was sad, not evil. Paumina believed that.

She had no time to waste. A trip into Dallas would take nearly two hours. If all went perfectly, she would still not make it back to Grand Saline by sundown. But it didn't matter how long it would take her, she had to go because she was useless in any other endeavor. She had to convince him.

The seats of the blue 1952 Mercury were warmed by the November sun on what proved to be a mild autumn day. Paumina set her handbag in the floor and slid her shoes off, kicking them back snuggly under the seat and out of her way. It was her usual way of setting out on a road trip, as ritual as Sunday communion. She felt more in control of the vehicle with her bare feet pressed on the pedals where she could feel them with her skin. That's how she had learned to drive years ago, and how she drove still.

She drove back from Dallas the same way, only much more at ease in her heart.

By eight o'clock, Vencher Thames had notified the State Police of the goings on in Grand Saline. Paumina felt with certainty that by nine o'clock Ben would be released from prison. Now all she had to do was drive back to the farm and tell Rhoda everything was going to be okay and to kiss her grandbaby girl's beautiful pudgy cheeks. She expected she'd be there by ten, maybe need to wake them from their sleep, but she had promised Ben she'd go. Better late than never.

14

As the very last drops of formula were sucked into Nanshe's mouth, Rhoda glanced again at the clock. It was only 6:30 and yet the sun had been set nearly an hour. Nanshe's hunger had seemed insatiable, as if she desperately needed something unidentifiable but all she knew to cry for was food. No matter how Rhoda held her, rocked her, gently bounced her, or sang to her; Nanshe cried until she was fed again. Rhoda wondered if she knew her Daddy was gone. But, how could a two month old infant know such things? Maybe she didn't know all the details, but knew that her daddy hadn't been the one to feed her in a very long time.

At least, this time, Nanshe fell asleep after finishing the bottle. She had fought sleep almost all day. Rhoda had barely had time to think about anything other than appeasing the child. She was relieved to finally see the tiny eyelids close and hear the sleepy sigh as the bottle was removed from Nanshe's lips. Rhoda carried the baby down the darkened hallway to the bassinet and laid her down.

Once Nanshe was settled, Rhoda's mind again turned to thoughts of Paumina and why she had not yet arrived. It was bad enough that she had lost faith in the police even allowing Ben a phone call at all. But, considering the telephone line had been disconnected somehow, she felt quite certain there was more going on than she dared imagine. Rhoda suspected that, even without a phone call, Paumina may show up after church just to check on Nanshe. Rhoda convinced herself all she needed to do was wait.

After the sun had set, she kept the house in the dark. Ben's warning was only to stay hidden. He had not told her to make the house look unoccupied, but she took that as a given. Maybe she was being overly cautious. Maybe her mind was twisting things. But, she kept the lights off just in case.

She sat on the bed where Ben would've been sleeping had he not been taken off to jail. Her eyes returned again and again to the pillow where she had previously found the shotgun. Curiosity took over and she reached over to slide her hand under it, wondering if Ben had replaced it there. Her fingers touched the stock causing adrenaline to make her heart skip. The feel of it reminded her of her pistol. She knew soon enough she would be leaving, returning to her original plan. She decided to gather her things together.

With only the light of the moon coming in the

windows, Rhoda went upstairs to gather her coat. On the bed lay a white nightgown. Ben must have placed it there earlier in the day. The moon reflected off the pearly white buttons down the center of the bodice. It was beautiful, so beautiful she wondered if it had been Della's. She quickly pushed the thought away. Ben would have never given it to her if it had belonged to his wife. It must have been extra clothes Paumina kept on hand.

She slid the shirtwaist dress off to her feet and pulled the nightgown over her head. It smelled strongly of cedar, which was reassuring. This nightgown had been stored for a long time.

Rhoda picked up her coat from the corner chair and headed down to the laundry room. She placed the green dress into a pile of unwashed clothes in the floor before going to the window to push open the curtains and let in the moonlight. She folded her clean, dry clothes as she removed them from the line and placed them into an oval wicker laundry basket. She carried it back to Ben's room and set it on the bed. She then felt between the mattresses until she found her pistol on the side of the bed where Della would have slept. She had meant to place the gun in the basket with her clothes, but the feel of it against the skin of her fingertips made her want to hug it to her chest. Her hand held the gun and shook as thoughts of shooting herself, right then and there, raged through her mind like a stampede of frightened animals.

Rhoda looked at the bassinet which contained a sleeping Nanshe and convinced herself to fight back the urge. She shoved the pistol into her coat pocket. To keep it close to her, she pulled the coat on over her nightgown. Her fingers smoothed over the outside of the coat, the fabric thick and rough. Her hand lingered at the feel the lump where the gun was concealed. Her fingers shook as she fumbled up to her breast pocket to check for the four bullets she had placed there earlier. They were held warm and dry.

She took a deep breath and sighed. Unable to stop herself, she pulled the pistol from her pocket and inserted all four bullets. When she snapped the chamber back in place, a sense of calm washed over her. Now, nothing would stand in her way. All she had to do was wait for Paumina to come.

She made her way to the kitchen where the clock indicated the time was eight o'clock. Evening service at the church should have been over already. Rhoda went to the back door and peered through the glass hoping to see headlights coming down the driveway. In the distance, she saw an orange glow in the darkness, like a flame but nothing like the headlights of a car. It was too small for Rhoda to tell what exactly it was. She stood still, captivated in her effort to identify it.

Only when she heard the front door slam did her concentration break. She walked to the living room expecting to see Paumina. Instead, she saw a man in a white robe, his face covered by a white pointed hat. Pale eyes, colorless in the shadows, stared back at her.

"Well, well," the man sneered, his voice young but not innocent. "I guess we've found that White woman dead in Ben Whitmer's house. We were going to burn it to the ground, but I'd hate to tamper with evidence."

Rhoda stood paralyzed. She had heard about the KKK her whole life and had heard rumors about a few people in her hometown being involved with them. But she had never seen a Klansman up close, certainly not dressed like a ghost. There had been a few boys back home who had bragged about harassing Blacks in other towns, but they were known liars and pathetic in general. She wondered if this man standing before her now was like them. Thinking he was made her marginally less afraid, but her heart still pounded and her mind raced to predict his next move.

He stepped closer to Rhoda, bringing himself more distinctly into view from the shadows. She could make out the color blue in his pale eyes as they peered out of the holes cut in the fabric. They were watery and bloodshot. Was he drunk?

"But we can't just find you dead." He gently touched the back of his hand to Rhoda's temple. He leaned forward and smelled what remained of her hair, inhaling deeply and holding it in. "Tell me, has he been fucking you?"

"No!" the word flew out of her in the high-pitched tone of a deceptive woman. She swallowed hard and tried to make sense of what was happening.

"Liar!" The man screamed and slapped the back of his hand against her cheek. Rhoda stumbled and tried to regain her balance; but before she could steady herself, the man knocked her onto the floor. "He fucked you and now you're full of animal seed, aren't you? Did you beg him for it, you filthy whore?"

The man stood to tower of her and kicked his boot into her ribs before she could move. Rhoda curled up to try to protect herself from the next kick, but the man had no intention of kicking her again. He was busily unfastening his belt. With his pants around his ankles and his robe raised about his waist, he fell on top of her. He held her wrists in his hands, stretching her arms out like a cross. His knees wedged between her legs, ripping the nightgown. She felt his naked penis against her, pushing to find its way in.

"I smell him on you," the man's voice was a sigh, "If I close my eyes it will be just like fucking his wife. But you won't fight me like she did, will you? You'll appreciate what a White man gives you."

Her stomach rolled with disgust and horror. She had no idea how she would get free. All she could think of was Nanshe and what would happen if they found her; at least, that's all she could think of until the man successfully entered her. At that moment, she lost all sense of being. She was nothing, no one, nowhere just as she had been as a little girl when her mother had pressed the red hot tip of a cigarette into her back. But the vacancy and blindness was short lived. She couldn't stay lost in insanity with the violent way her stomach churned with a need to vomit. The tightening of her throat and the need to swallow repeatedly to keep it down had ripped her back into the reality of what was happening. Tears burned her eyes as her mouth clamped closed. The pain of something solid, like a rock, pressing into her hip and commanded all her attention. She realized it was the barrel of her pistol tucked beneath her. The solution to ending the attack was so close, yet seemed impossibly far away.

Rhoda forced a moan of fake pleasure from her lips. She hoped the man would not look at her and see the tears running from her eyes as she whispered, "Yes, yes…" by his ear. She felt him relax his grip as he sighed in response and leaned his covered head onto her shoulder. The white fabric smelled unexpectedly floral like freshly washed hair. She wondered if he had come from church. Again, Rhoda pictured her mother. No one knew how terrible she had truly been.

Rhoda didn't waste time thinking more about it. She sighed and breathed on his neck where it was exposed between the flaps of his hood. She took the lobe of his ear between her teeth and sighed again, more convincingly passionate. She kissed his neck, stealthily fighting back down the contents of her stomach which rose again and again into her throat.

The man slid his hands from Rhoda's wrists to cup her breasts beneath the weight of his own chest. He handled them roughly, adding to the pain of her already tender tissue. Rhoda struggled to maintain the deception of pleasure. She needed it to end soon. She continued to kiss his neck and ear to keep him from moving his head. She didn't want him to turn and see her hand sliding into her coat pocket. She grasped the the pistol with determination at the same moment her milk was coaxed to release by ignorant, barbaric hands. Rhoda ran her other hand up into his hair beneath the hood and pressed his head to the side of her face as she encouraged him, "Yes, yes!"

She tried to keep his focus off the wetness growing between their chests as she lifted the pistol to the exact spot on his skull where a day earlier she had planned to shoot her own. Without a moment of hesitation, she pulled the trigger. The sound of the shot was deafening. Simultaneously, Rhoda felt the man's skull break apart against her. The man's body jerked above her in spasms before dropping its full dead weight onto her chest.

A sharp pain stung Rhoda's ear and her lungs fought to pull air under his weight. His warm blood pooled beneath her head which was the last horror Rhoda could endure. She shoved the body off of her and rolled over to vomit onto the floor. She heaved again and again until it hurt her muscles to continue. Blood dripped down over her face until it ran off her nose. Her ear burned with intense pain. Not all of the blood was his.

Many minutes passed before she registered the sound of Nanshe crying.

15

Rhoda ran to the bathroom sink and splashed water over her face. Blood, his and hers, ran red down her arms, the sight of which caused her stomach to clench. She vomited over the toilet, but nothing came. She went back to the sink and pushed her head beneath the water, holding her breath as she tried to rinse away the gruesomeness without accidentally ingesting it. She lifted her head and gasped for air before clamping her mouth closed once again. She shook her head and grabbed the towel from the bar and dried herself frantically. Clumps of bone and clots of blood were still stuck in her hair and came loose onto the pale green towel. Rhoda scrubbed to clear her hair as best she could.

Tossing the towel onto the floor, Rhoda ran to the

back bedroom. The clothes basket from earlier still set on the bed. She quickly tossed a couple of Nanshe's sleepers and a handful of cloth diapers into it. She pulled out the nightstand drawer and dumped the contents into the basket, then swept in everything from atop it. Rhoda opened dresser drawers, one after the other, ruffling through the clothing items, looking for something she couldn't define. In the bottom drawer was a zippered pouch which jingled with coins and a large envelope so full of documents it could no longer be sealed. Rhoda tossed them both into the basket.

On top of it all, she laid Nanshe's three baby blankets and straightened them as quickly as should could. Nanshe still wailed. When Rhoda turned to lift her from the bassinet, a bright light from outside the window caught her eye. Rhoda stepped closer and saw the light was emanating from a huge fire. The entire barn was ablaze. Rhoda felt in her gut that whoever burned the barn would eventually come for the house. She pictured Henry and Benoni as she had imagined them when Ben had told her their story. She thought of all they had put into building up the farm and how quickly it could be lost, and would be lost, if she didn't do something.

She left Nanshe crying in the bassinet and pulled the shotgun from under the pillow. She slid the window up and immediately heard the frantic cries of sheep in the distance. They were lucky to have been out in the field at the moment Ben had been arrested and so were now free to escape the fire. Rhoda leaned low, peering out the window at the distinct sight of pointed white hoods. Shadows and orange glow flickered against their robes causing them to look like demons in the night. Rhoda thought of the dead man's body on the living room floor, his head broken open and his blood running out onto the half-century old rug. She raised the shotgun to the window opening and steadied herself. Just like taking careful aim at a groundhog in the garden back in Tennessee, she took in a slow, deep breath and held it, centered her target, and pulled the trigger.

The startling sound of the gunfire momentarily silenced Nanshe's screams. Immediately, Rhoda's targeted man fell to his knees before falling forward face down on the ground. As if too afraid to scream, Nanshe remained silent as two other men ran toward the fallen man outside on the lawn. One held a lit torch in his hand, the other pulled a pistol from under his robe. While the man with the torch bent over the fallen man, the one with the pistol scanned the darkened night. His eyes squinted toward the house as the only logical place to look for the shooter, but he did not immediately realize the darkened bedroom window had been opened slightly. He did not see the the barrel of the shotgun pointed in his direction. Nor did he hear the sound of Rhoda's second shot until he felt the sting in his arm. By the time he realized he had been hit, the next shot pierced his neck causing his head to nearly separate from his body.

Rhoda watched him fall with an eerie satisfaction.

The man who was bent over the first man began to call out into the night. Rhoda knew there were more men, but could make no guess as to how many or where they were located. She quickly aimed to take out the third man, but he had already begun to run to the west out of her sight.

Nanshe's grunts were small as she built up her courage to cry again. Rhoda set the shotgun on the bed and lifted Nanshe up from the bassinet and placed her into the laundry basket. Lifting it, Rhoda realized it was heavier than she expected now that it was full of what she hoped were important things. Regardless, it was too late to take out anything. Rhoda picked up the shot gun and placed it under her arm. She needed a free hand to snag a photo from the end table in the living room. It was a photo of Ben and Della on her wedding day.

After a quick pass in and out of the living room, she made her way to the kitchen where three nails were left sticking out of the wall by the back door. Each was for a different set of keys. Paumina's were missing. She took both sets of keys from the two remaining nails and ran out into the night toward Ben's truck. Nanshe screamed as loudly as the first time Rhoda had heard her, sheep baaed and screamed in the distant darkness, a loud roaring with pops and cracks came from the burning barn wood, and Rhoda's legs moved faster than they had ever moved before.

She opened the (thankfully unlocked) passenger door and set the basket on the straight seat of the truck. She pulled the seatbelt around it and clicked it in place hoping to keep the basket secured. After slamming the door shut, she ran around to the driver's side while her fingers flipped through the keys hoping to catch hold of just the right one.

A shot was heard, fired from the direction of the burning barn. Rhoda jumped into the driver's seat and tried to slide the first key into the ignition. It didn't fit. She fumbled for the next key and tried it, only then looking up to see three men running through a field in the distance, lit torches burning. Rhoda leaned over and locked Nanshe's door, then her own. She kept her eyes on the burning torches coming ever closer as she shoved one key after another to the opening of the ignition. She lost count of how many times it failed. She was certain she was going back over the same keys again. Was she even turning them the right way?

"Come on!" She pleaded in a whisper.

The men reached the fence surrounding the pasture and were hiking up their robes to climb over it. Rhoda reached down and picked up the shotgun from the floorboard where she had set it while buckling Nanshe. With it across her lap, she resumed her attempt to find the right key. Finally, a key slipped into place.

Rhoda froze with stunned relief; her hands trembled as she turned the switch and heard the motor roar to life. Without even looking for the headlight switch, she jammed the truck into gear and pressed her foot down onto the gas pedal with all her might. The truck lurched forward into the yard. With Nanshe's screams drowning out Rhoda's own thoughts, she gained speed while bumping over the ruts in the grass. The wide-eyed men on the fence were busily trying to get their costumed selves over the fence either toward her or away, any way as long as it was off their vulnerable perch. Two of the men made it down barely long enough for their feet to hit the ground before Rhoda rammed the truck into them.

The third man was the only man she heard make a sound as he screamed in fear just before his legs were slammed by the grill. His body was thrown into the air, but the truck still moved forward with all the power Rhoda could give. The man's body came crashing down onto the roof of the truck. A dent popped down by Rhoda's head before she heard him land in the truck bed.

All the loud noises had once again brought Nanshe to silence, or perhaps the baby was reassessing the success of her methods. What had worked a few hours earlier was no longer earning her a bottle of milk and only seemed to initiate chaos.

Rhoda spun the truck around in the pasture, no sheep in sight because even sheep knew when to get out of the way. She turned her headlights on and aimed the truck back out the break in the fence where she had just crashed through. She knew there would be bodies of dead or dying men sprawled in her path. In her mind, she screamed at them in a way she dared not do aloud in front of Nanshe. You do not belong here! No one invited you! You killed an innocent mother and an innocent man is taking the blame! You are evil and deserve to die!

Even under all the duress, her brain didn't miss an opportunity to taunt her. It remind her that her words to the men also applied to herself. Rhoda was not invited. She did not belong. She came to kill an innocent mother, herself. And if she had done that, Ben would have been blamed for her death. A sick feeling washed over her as she realized the extent of the hatred Ben must have felt toward her. She understood his reasons because, at that moment, even Rhoda hated herself. She hated every common trait she shared with those evil men. She hated her ignorance for having thought, just a day ago, that she could blow her head off and there would be no consequences for others.

Now the consequences for others would be too great for Rhoda to even think of suicide. She knew it was still be only a matter of time before the thoughts returned, but she felt sure it would be no time soon. Nanshe needed her.

She had already driven down the long dirt driveway and onto a paved road before she realized she had nowhere to go. Even if she knew where Paumina was staying, she wasn't sure if it was safe to go there. Whoever was responsible for the attack on Ben's property would have likely planned for what to do about Paumina. They may have even planned on her being at Ben's house when they arrived. She shuddered at the thought. She preferred to think the men believed Paumina would have Nanshe in town and the farm would be empty for them to ransack and destroy. But, remembering that the phone line had been disconnected made Rhoda doubt that assumption. Most likely, those men meant to leave no trace of the Whitmers or their history.

Rhoda wondered if any of the men had recognized her. Would the police be looking for Ben's truck? How long did she have until the cops were notified? One thing was certain, she couldn't trust anyone until she crossed the Van Zandt county line. Maybe she'd have to get out of Texas altogether. She had no idea if she was even headed in the right direction, but soon the town of Grand Saline came into view. As she approached the first brick building on her right, she held her breath and hoped the roar of the truck would not draw attention. She wanted to press hard on the gas pedal to carry them in and out of the town before anyone noticed, but thought it best to stay as slow and quiet as possible. For a moment, she even considered turning off the headlights but thought that would make her look even more suspicious.

A few intersections later, the road met up with a highway with signs pointing east and west. She didn't know where exactly she was in the state of Texas, or which way to go. But she had already traveled through the towns east of Grand Saline on the bus. Everything had looked the same, and at that moment, Rhoda wanted anything but more of the same. She pulled the steering wheel to the right and headed west.

16

Thoughts were loose strings Rhoda's mind whipped into a frenzy until they began to tangle into unmanageable knots. She felt the weight of the mass in her head spinning as if rolling down a hill in a box, going too fast, hitting the ground and up and around and crashing back down. Her heart raced with fear and regret, anticipation and moments of panic. The ideas, memories, and images playing out in her mind came so quickly and evolved so often that Rhoda felt she had been thinking them for hours and hours. But she had only been driving for ten minutes.

Because it seemed she had been lost in thought for hours, Rhoda was startled when she realized she had not heard a sound from Nanshe in (what felt like) hours. As she had commonly done with Olivia, Rhoda reached out her hand to gently place it on Nanshe's chest hoping to feel the rise and fall of a tiny ribcage. Not know exactly which way beneath the mound of warm blankets the baby was facing, Rhoda slid her hand over the lump until she felt it move. Under the weight of Rhoda's hand, the heap of blanket shuddered. Rhoda heard Nanshe sigh and breathe again, this time through her mouth with the faintest hint of a snore.

Rhoda's heart broke a little more knowing Nanshe had likely given up hope of anyone helping her. Nanshe had soothed herself to sleep when Rhoda should have been the one to care for her, feed her hungry belly, and embrace her to let her know she was not alone. But Rhoda reasoned with herself that there was nothing she could have done while trying to save their lives. Still, the guilt lingered, pricking her brain, adding to the chorus of other wrongs Rhoda felt incapable of righting.

But she did not feel guilty about shooting the men from the window, or ramming into the men on the fence. She thought of her actions as if they had all been a dream. Flashes of memory came out of order, the man falling to the ground, the jostling of the truck as it rammed the fence, filling the basket with random mementos and supplies, the feel of the rifle steadied against her shoulder. She thought of everything except the man who had assaulted her in the living room. That memory was absent, pushed into a dark box and locked away because even the memory of it would threaten Rhoda's survival.

It's strange how the brain works this way. Rhoda had the memory, and yet she didn't, not at that moment as she drove down highway 80. Her mind was full of what if, still contemplating what would have happened if she had not gathered Nanshe's things, had not shot the men at the barn, had not rammed the fence. What if. Rhoda considered all the terrible possibilities, all that might have happened to cause Paumina's absence, and all that might happen to Ben if she didn't find help.

Not fifteen minutes after crossing the Grand Saline line, Nanshe began to cry again. Rhoda was not about to let the child cry herself to sleep again. She pulled the truck to the side of the road and turned off the headlights. She unbuttoned her nightgown in a daze of adrenaline and mental exhaustion, and lifted Nanshe from the basket. It was only when Nanshe began to nurse that Rhoda remembered what had happened in the living room. A tiny flash of memory, the feel of the man's hands on her breasts, was all it took to make Rhoda physically sick. She wanted to wash herself and felt terrible that Nanshe had to drink milk from a breast which had been made so dirty. While her mind beat itself with the thoughts of her filthiness, her mothering hormones triggered feelings of bliss so out of place that the combination caused Rhoda to nearly black out entirely. She felt the air around her thicken until she could barely breathe it in. Her thoughts and emotions were killing her. She needed a place that felt safe from the chaos inside herself, some thought to keep her from truly losing her sanity. But the only thought that came close to doing that was the one involving the pistol in her coat pocket.

Rhoda leaned her head against the truck's back window and imagined her skull exploding, beautifully breaking to bits. Rhoda sighed and took a deep, calming breath and pictured it again. And again. Boom. Shatter. Thoughts fading. Boom. Shatter.

When a blinding light shone red through her closed

eyelids, Rhoda opened them to see a train coming right at her. Only when it was a few feet away did she realize it would pass beside the parked truck and she was not about to die. But, the moment of panic was the last thing she needed. Her stomach churned and she felt a thickness in her throat.

She pulled the door handle to open the truck door and, with Nanshe held close, she slid from the truck and bent over to vomit in the ditch. Her legs shook so badly she had to kneel down and there she vomited again. Nanshe clung to Rhoda's nightgown and her tiny fingernails scratched at Rhoda's skin to get a better grasp as Rhoda's body convulsed in an effort to purge every bad feeling from within her gut.

Rhoda wanted water, but had none. She wiped at her mouth as she cried, feeling sorry for herself. She wiped her cheeks with the sleeve of her coat and tried to pull herself together. She made it back to her feet and steadied herself when she realized Nanshe had stopped nursing. Rhoda looked down at her in the darkness and saw the baby girl looking back up at her, grinning. Rhoda forced a smile in return, though she wasn't sure if Nanshe was giving her a real smile or if it was just gas. Soon, the answer came loudly from beneath Nanshe's sleeper. The baby needed a change.

"Okay," Rhoda sighed, "Your timing, kid, is not great. But I delayed your eating schedule. You might as well delay my escape-and-not-get-murdered-by-the-KKK schedule."

She walked to the seat of the truck on the passenger side. There was very little natural light, but Rhoda was determined to change Nanshe in the dark. She was afraid to turn on lights and draw attention to Ben's truck. She needed to be quick. She laid Nanshe back in the basket so she could use both hands to lower it into the floorboard. She lifted Nanshe out again and with one hand placed a blanket on the truck seat, then laid Nanshe on it. Rhoda worked quickly to get the baby cleaned up and changed. Afterward, she was left with many dirty things and had no way to launder them or even store them.

She hugged Nanshe, now clean and dressed, to her chest with one arm while the other folded up the blanket around the dirty laundry. She decided to throw it into the back of the truck; but when her arm was midway over the edge of the truck bed, she caught sight of the body of a man in a white robe. His legs were twisted in an impossible way; the sight of them made Rhoda feel sick again. Regardless, she couldn't take her eyes off it. These men had not seemed real in their robes flecked with orange firelight. She wanted to take a closer look.

Carefully she placed Nanshe back into the basket, now on the floor of the truck, and covered her with a blanket. With the baby safely away from the gruesome sight, Rhoda walked slowly around to the tailgate and dropped it gently to reveal the blood soaked white hood of one of the many men she had killed, or tried to, that night.

Looking at the hood made her mind pulse with images of the man she had shot in Ben's living room. Her brain switched them interchangeably until she was no longer sure if the man in the back of the truck was from the fence or from the living room. She felt her sanity slipping and struggled to hold onto it for Nanshe's sake. She thought, maybe if she looked at the man's face the nightmare playing over in her head would stop. She wanted to see this man, make him more than a ghost or a monster in the night.

With a shaking hand, she reached out for the fabric of the hood and before she could talk herself out of it, she yanked it off the man's head. As if poisonous to her skin, she dropped the hood onto the ground and wiped her hands on the front of her coat. Her preoccupation with wiping off the contamination had caused her to not notice that the man's silvery eyes were open and focused on her. It wasn't until he spat blood from between his broken teeth that she realized he was not dead.

A gasp, not a scream, escaped Rhoda's mouth before she covered it. She might have been surprised, but her fear of drawing attention to herself overrode her fear of the mangled man. She leaned closer to look at him, trying to make out what he might have looked like before she had hit him with the truck. He was an older man with a narrow face, a short gray beard, and thin cracked lips.

"Bitch!" He breathed out the word with great effort, then spit again. "Damn Negro-lovin' traitor!"

The man's upper body shook with effort as he attempted to move. It occurred to Rhoda that he may have a gun. She shoved her hand inside her coat pocket and felt the pistol. Her fingers wrapped around it as a tingling sensations pulsed through her veins.

The man breathed in a raspy breath and exhaled his words in short phrases. "If you... were a good... woman... you would... drop that baby... on the train... track... like a rabid... dog."

Rhoda's mind flashed images of her daughter's bloated body after it had been pulled from the river. That was what Ed had wanted. He had thought Olivia would be better dead than alive. If Rhoda had not tolerated him, Olivia would have lived. Now, Rhoda wished she had shot Ed just like she had shot those men on Ben's lawn. She wished she had killed him long before he had a chance to kill Olivia.

Before she knew what she was doing, she had aimed the pistol at the face of the Klansman. Only when he began to laugh did she snap out of her fantasy. But only a small piece of her mind seemed to register that she was not back in time. Her body still seemed to be locked into the dream of shooting Ed. She wanted to fire the weapon and watch his head explode. She wanted that for Ed and she wanted that for the Klansman. She wanted to erase them both for the evil within them. As if she had made a logical decision, though there was nothing logical about her at that moment, she pulled the trigger. The deafening sound of the shot happened a split second after the bullet entered the man's silvery eye and popped out the back of his head leaving a trail of bone and brains across the truck bed.

Rhoda blinked, trying to gain clarity. But none came. She was completely overcome with anger and bitterness at the loss of her child which seemed one and the same as the loss of Della, the arrest of Ben, the suffering of Nanshe, and the burning of a hundred year old farm. Was the house still standing? She had no way of knowing, but in her mind, it was gone. All of it was gone.

She slammed closed the tailgate and climbed into the driver's seat. She started the engine, her teeth clenched with determination. She pulled out onto the road with a sharp turn, her tires squealing as she whipped the truck around to face back toward Grand Saline.

17

Rhoda drove along the streets of downtown Grand Saline looking for the police department. Without any police cars parked along the streets, the only indication that she had found it was the City Hall sign above a door. The small, one level brick building was newer than the surrounding buildings. The brick was painted white and looked delicate with its large windows and cream colored blinds. It hugged up to an old saloon type structure to the west. To the east was the corner of Frank and Green. The police station doors faced out to Green.

There were parking places designated for Police vehicles, but none were present. Rhoda figured they were probably all out at Ben's farm cleaning up bodies and putting out fires. Maybe some of those men trying to burn

Ben's farm had actually been police officers. Rhoda imagined they were frantically trying to frame Ben for the killings and the fire, or maybe they would frame Paumina (wherever she was). But there was one dead body they couldn't tamper with or hide. She was going to plant it at their door and hope the entire town would look at it and feel ashamed for what had taken place that night. But for all she knew, the whole town was in on it.

She turned the truck around and backed it up to the doors of the police station. The area was lit by a single streetlight at the corner. Still full of adrenaline and determination, she shifted into park and killed the headlights. Stepping out of the truck, she felt the glow of the streetlight like a spotlight beaming down from the wide open Texas sky. There was an eerie sense that she was being watched, as if on stage. She almost hoped someone was watching her to see what evil men deserver. But she couldn't shake the feeling that the eyes she felt were those of Grandma Vickers.

She walked to the back of the truck and opened the tailgate. Blood dripped out over the dusty chrome bumper and onto the sidewalk. Disgusted by the sight of the body, she hesitated almost imperceptibly before grabbing the dead man's feet. She gave them a firm tug, but found it unexpectedly difficult to slide the body out of the truck bed. As she struggled, her skin began to crawl with a feeling of contamination. With every repositioning of her hands and every slip of her fingers, time began to close in on her. The poison of evilness pricked her skin and made her feel numb. She didn't want to touch it anymore. And as much as she wanted to send a message to the town, the last thing she wanted was to get caught in the act and have Nanshe handed over to those horrible people.

"Damn it," she sighed and dropped the leg she'd been pulling. She ran back to the driver's seat and pulled the door closed behind her.

"Hold on," she said in the direction of the basket on the floor. Nanshe was sleeping there, wrapped in a warm blanket.

Rhoda looked straight ahead and focused into the darkness. She gripped the steering wheel so hard her knuckles turned white. She reached down and shifted into first gear before slamming down the gas pedal. The truck jerked forward, tires squealing. In the rearview mirror she saw the jostling of the body as it hit the ground and came to a rest ten feet from the police department doors. Her eyes darted to focus in front of her just in time to see she was speeding toward a railroad embankment. She slammed on the brakes and turned the steering wheel sharply to the right. The truck bounced halfway up the slope but managed to circle back to the road without tipping over.

Her hands tingled with numbness and shock, her palms were clammy. Dead silence filled the cab of the truck as she rolled to a stop on a back road behind the downtown buildings. A full minute passed before her ears began to ring and then pulse with the beat of her terrified heart. It felt like forever had passed. She had nearly killed herself and Nanshe both.

Just when Rhoda's mind pulled together enough to think about what to do next, Nanshe began to whimper. In seconds, her whimpers grew into a full cry. Nanshe seemed so upset that Rhoda thought she may have been injured in the near accident they had just experienced.

Rhoda pulled the truck over to the grass along the road and parked there under a post oak tree. She turned off the engine and hoped, for a moment, she would fade into the scenery. She needed to tend to Nanshe. After everything the baby had been through, Rhoda could not ask her to wait once again.

As she scooped up Nanshe from the basket, little legs kicked and arms punched the air. Screams and grunts combined as she arched her tiny back in protest. The blanket dropped free from Rhoda's grasp and she let it fall. The sooner Rhoda could get Nanshe to latch and drink, the sooner she would be soothed and quiet. There was no thought given to her own trauma or the way her body reacted last time Nanshe nursed. She hugged Nanshe close to keep her from flailing out of her grasp while she unbuttoned her nightgown, but her nightgown was already unbuttoned from the time before.

Memories flooded in, but she pushed them away as she tried to position the screaming child against her breast. Rhoda was sure the feel of skin would bring her out of her fit and soon she would latch. But Nanshe only screamed louder and turned her head away from Rhoda.

"Shhh," she bounced the baby gently and rocked her in her arms. She turned her so the baby's belly pressed against her and tried again to get her to drink. Nanshe screamed and pushed away, twisted her head to the side, and kicked her feet against Rhoda's arm so hard that Rhoda nearly lost her grip.

"What is it?" Rhoda demanded as softly as she could. Tears came to her eyes. "Do you not want me?"

Rhoda's voice could not be heard over the cries, but she convinced herself it had not only been heard but also answered. Nanshe did not want her. She wanted her Daddy.

"That's how it should be," Rhoda said aloud. She

wiped her tears from her cheeks. "Of course you want your Daddy, but he isn't here. It's only me and I'm doing the best I can. Shhh...."

Still, nothing Rhoda did soothed Nanshe. Ten minutes of trying to pacify the child felt like ten hours. Rhoda's willpower was breaking. She tried everything she could to comfort and calm Nanshe, but nothing worked. With all her focus on Nanshe, Rhoda had stopped paying attention to the state of her own mind. She did not fight so hard to keep the ruinous thoughts out of her head. Every few seconds she would black out completely, but so briefly she convinced herself to ignore it. Everything was going to be okay. She could handle it. She had handled it before, hadn't she?

And with that thought, Rhoda slipped into her destructive memories like being sucked into a tornado of guilt, grief, and shame.

18

Meanwhile, a few miles from downtown Grand Saline, the fires at Ben's farm burned on like the fires of Hell. But Van Zandt County Sheriff Orrin Creager didn't know about them. He only knew about Ben's problematic arrest. He had been informed of the details by a call from the Governor. Though Orrin Creager and Rob Bowlin had been friends for thirty years, there was no way he was going to suffer the consequences of ignoring a call from Governor. So Sheriff Creager had personally set out toward Grand Saline, after dark as it was, to talk one on one with Police Chief Bowlin. Friend or not, he was not willing to see his career come to an end over Rob Bowlin's antics.

Orrin remembered Rob from high school and was

well aware of his involvement in the KKK. But he never took them seriously back then. Orrin was too busy with school and his efforts to get a football scholarship to give much thought to what Rob was getting into. To Orrin, the KKK just seemed like rabble-rousers, full of ego but not really hurting anyone.

Now he wasn't so sure. He hoped he would be able to talk some sense into Rob, convince him to let that Black man go back to his farm in peace. Maybe the governor would be satisfied with that. But Orrin suspected there was more to the story, a story of which he truly wanted no part. Obviously, a murder of a Black woman had occurred and someone had to be guilty, if not that Ben Whitmer man, than someone else. Orrin hoped like Hell Rob wasn't the one to blame. If there was a way, he'd try to help clean up the mess and sweep it all out of sight. But if that didn't look likely, Rob would have to pay for what he'd done. Orrin hated that, but had to accept the possibility of choosing between a friendship and his job.

At a half past nine o'clock, Orrin turned left onto a road leading to Grand Saline. He expected to arrive just before ten. He turned on the radio to hear Buck Owen's new song, "Tall Dark Stranger". Orrin leaned back in his seat and propped his arm up on the headrest of the passenger seat. He began to sing along, imagining himself being the tall dark stranger, creeping into Grand Saline to attract the longing eyes of the ladies. He tapped his fingers and bobbed his head and took his dreams another step further. Why pretend to be Orrin Creager attracting ladies when he could imagine being Buck Owens himself?

Yes, going back to Grand Saline always made Orrin

feel young and invincible. Not even his worries about the governor could keep him from his fantasies.

19

"Stop it!" Rhoda screamed. "Just stop!"

If anyone had been outside the truck they would have sworn Rhoda was screaming at Nanshe. But Rhoda was actually screaming at her own mind. Inside, a motion picture spun through a reel to reel at an unendurable speed. Cigarettes, clumps of loose hair, baby dolls, calloused hands, sewing needles stitching holes, laughing cousins, white hoods, rain on tall June tobacco, Ben's kiss, burning barn, the clean smell of shampoo, the sound of crying sheep in the darkness.

"Make it stop!" Her tears rolled down her cheeks. She hugged Nanshe against her shoulder and wanted the little girl to hug her back. She needed the impossible. Nanshe was too young. She was powerless to comfort

Rhoda even if somehow she had wanted to do so. Nanshe couldn't even comfort herself. All they could do was scream together into the night as if someone was out there to fix their brokenness.

Rhoda rubbed Nanshe's back and focused on stopping her own tears.

"I don't think anyone's going to save us," She conceded, but thought for a moment. "Well, there is always your Daddy," she sniffed to try to gain her composure. "If he could hear you, he would save you, baby girl. He would love you. But, I have nobody at all. It doesn't matter how much I scream now. No one's going to rock me and tell me shhh. No one's even going to think about that."

Rhoda patted the baby's back firmly, hoping the crying was due to gas. Her earlier attempts to burp her had failed. Rhoda was just cycling through everything her instincts told her to do to calm a crying child. Nothing was working. Nothing.

"You need him. That's what this is, I know. You don't want this murdering woman. You want your fine Daddy. You're scared of me, aren't you?"

Nanshe's crying kept her from hearing anything Rhoda said, not that she would have responded anyway. But the absence of any sign that her words were heard unnerved Rhoda even more. All of the strength she had been hoarding like precious food in a famine was being sucked out of her with every screaming second that ticked by.

"I'm afraid of me, too," Rhoda confessed. With a shaking hand she reached for the blanket and wrapped it as best she could around Nanshe. She fought to contain the little kicking legs and flailing arms until she had finally wrapped her in a tight cocoon. Nanshe's face was all that was visible, a wet with tears and puffy from crying face. Her cries persisted, though quieter through raspy and hoarse vocal chords. Rhoda wanted to lean forward and kiss her forehead but she suspected it would upset Nanshe even more, so she didn't.

"Let's go get your Daddy," she whispered. "I can't make you happy, but I can give you what you want."

With Nanshe hugged tightly in her left arm, Rhoda slid her right hand into her coat pocket. Despite already knowing it was there, she was startled by the feel of the gun. It felt alive, responding to her touch with electricity that raced through her. She curved her fingers around it and held it, felt it merge with her body to become just an extension of her arm. She was aware of how sad it was to feel completed by a weapon capable of destroying her. But she felt it none the less.

The pistol was part of her; but would it be enough to help her do what she needed to do to free Ben? The shotgun was another alternative. It laid in the floorboard of the truck where it had been forgotten until now. At most, it had two shots remaining. She wasn't sure if Ben had fully loaded it again after taking it from her in his field. She remembered that moment and how she had envied his wife for being dead. She still did. If she could bring Della back and take her place in the dark silence of death, she would. But envy would not help her through what was to come.

She pulled the pistol from her pocket and with a single motion dropped it into the basket on the floor and scooped up the shotgun. She placed it on the seat while she opened up the truck door. Then she retrieved it again before sliding out into the increasingly cool night air.

Nanshe breathed in a quick breath and exhaled a shuddering sigh of surrender. Once again, her needs had gone unmet. Rhoda breathed in a deep breath of her own, taking in the stillness along with the oxygen filling her lungs. She exhaled as she leaned against the side of the truck.

She wondered if she would be making this decision to rescue Ben if Nanshe had stopped crying five minutes earlier.

"That's the wrong question," she whispered up to the stars above her. The sky was clear and beautiful, infinite, and nothing like the cramped up space and time where she stood in Grand Saline. There was really only one way out for all of us. The timing may vary, but the conclusion is always the same.

The road was quiet except for the sound of Rhoda's feet. Her soft-soled shoes would have been nearly undetectable except for the occasional moments when she neglected to lift her foot high enough and it slid over tiny gravel. When she turned the corner onto Green Street and saw the streetlight a couple blocks away, she paused and took a breath.

She tried to imagine what would happen next. She wanted to know with certainty, but there wasn't much to be had. Ben would surely be upset with her. She would have to make it clear to the police officer, if one was even present, that this was all her own idea. If no officer was in the building, Ben may refuse to leave for fear of making things worse. She decided she would make him take Nanshe and leave. She had a gun. She could make him go. And then she would leave a note saying it was all her own idea. And then she would do what she came to Grand Saline to do in the first place.

Part of her regretted not doing it sooner, getting it over with before Ben had found her in his field. Yes, it would have caused him trouble, but the police were already framing him for murder. They were already going to arrest him no matter what. If she hadn't come inside the house, Paumina would have never left it. How would Paumina have handled the men in white robes? Had she had to deal with them before? Rhoda wasn't sure. Different scenarios played out in her mind. Maybe Paumina would have left with Nanshe and not even been there when the men came. Maybe Paumina would have shot them all on her own. Or, they could have killed Paumina and Nanshe both. Rhoda wasn't sure if she was the destroyer or the savior. As soon as she posed the question to herself, the answer was clear. She had never saved anything in her life. All she was doing now was cleaning up the mess she made.

20

As Rhoda stood in the shadows at the end of Green Street looking up toward the streetlight by the police station, a police car pulled around the corner and parked in front of the doors. A man got out and ran to the body sprawled in the center of the road. He squatted down beside it before leaning over it, touching it and shaking it as if somehow the faceless corpse would come back to life. The man arched his back and looked up to the sky, he shook his hands into the night and cried. Even from a distance Rhoda could discern the stretching of the fabric over the protruding belly of Police Chief Rob Bowlin.

Fortunately for Rhoda, he did not see her. He was too blinded by rage to see much of anything. Even as he had driven into Grand Saline, he had been so consumed with grief and dreams of vengeance and that he had barely kept sight of the road. That hunger to bring retribution was only magnified by the sight of his dead brother laid out like roadkill in front of the police station. He could not imagine how Paumina got the body there, but he was certain it had to have been her to do it. He was going to make Ben Whitmer pay.

Back at the Whitmer farm, all of his men were busy pulling robes off dead men and tossing them into the house in preparation to burn it all to the ground. Any evidence that they had instigated the night's events must be destroyed. With his men preoccupied, Rob had taken off in the police car to fetch Ben. Now there was a new situation to clean up, one he wasn't sure he was up for. He fully intending to make Ben assist in that cleanup. Ben needed literal blood on his hands to match what metaphorically already existed. Ben needed to suffer before Rob threw him in the fire. Paumina needed to pay, too. Seeing his brother dead solidified his resolve to find her and make that happen.

He had never expected a little old woman like Paumina to open fire. He was shocked even more to see she had killed a man inside the home she held so dear. He never questioned his belief that Paumina was the shooter. Rob had no reason to suspect the White woman Ben had called about would have stayed behind with the Whitmers. He had pushed the thought of that woman's existence out of his mind long ago. In Rob's world, White women simply did not associate with Black men; and they certainly didn't shoot White men from darkened windows. So it was Paumina Rob wanted to punish now more than ever. If he had known were she had driven off to, he'd have hunted her down instead of coming for Ben.

Initially, Rob had thought of Ben as a more suitable scapegoat. But no matter what the cost or how long it took him, he vowed he would see Paumina ripped apart for what she had done to his brother. Rob smiled with anticipation of the pain he was going to inflict, but his eyes still held their storm.

He stood and brushed the dust from his gray pants but never looked up into the darkness. He walked straight to the police station door and slid his key into the lock. It opened swiftly.

"Ben! Get up, boy!" Rob slapped the wall by the door a couple of times. "Your house is going up in flames and I'm sending you in to fight it to your death. Are you ready to fight fire, boy?"

Rob flipped the switch to the overhead light. Ben was in the back of the building in a jail cell. He saw the light come through the window of the door between the office and the jail. He had been sitting on the bed, awake in the dark, unable to sleep, nearly crazed with worry. He had known something terrible was happening, could feel it in the pit of his stomach. But hearing that his house was on fire made his heart nearly implode. Where was Nanshe? He couldn't bring himself to think of it. What they had done to Della was so terrible, his mind would not allow him to imagine that fate for his daughter. But even after banishing it from his mind, his body still reacted with nausea and shock.

The door between the office and jail cells flew open by the kick of Rob's boot. It slammed the wall behind it with a thud and bounced back toward Rob. His hand shot up to prevent it from hitting him. Then he just stood there, a silhouette against the light of the office. Ben held his saliva in his mouth, wanting Rob to come close enough to aim the spit directly between his eyes. It was the only weapon Ben had and could serve no purpose other than venting anger and starting a war he could not expect to win. Still, he pictured in a flash all the things he wanted to do to Rob if he would just come a little closer.

But Ben felt uneasy about the powerful craving for vengeance taking over his mind. He forced it back, swallowed it down, restrained his thoughts. He needed to be free. Blowing up in the heat of the moment would not get him out of that jail cell. Chief Bowlin could surely not get away with his actions forever. In the end he would have to pay, wouldn't he? Ben had to believe justice would eventually come if he could just make it through this alive long enough to see it.

Ben tried to hold his voice steady, "I'm not going anywhere until I speak to my lawyer."

"You ain't got a lawyer, boy! You used your one call to call your mommy. And now she's gone and attacked my officers. And unfortunately for the both of you, she killed my brother. It's time to pay. When I find her, I'll kill her slow, one piece at a time." Rob laughed maniacally. "But right now I have to take care of Grand Saline's only Negro firefighter."

Something didn't sound right to Ben. Paumina was not a gunslinger and there was no mention of Rhoda or Nanshe. Too many possibilities flooded Ben's mind, some of them so terrible they nearly swallowed him up. He tried to stay focused on what he knew for sure. The police had been at his house. Shots were fired. His house was on fire, or would be. He was about to be taken home, likely to be killed while being framed for whatever happened there. Part of him wanted to play along just to get back home and get more information for himself. Another part

133

of him wanted to crush Chief Bowlin's skull, steal the police car, and go find his mother and daughter. What if Nanshe's already dead? The thought sucked the fight out of him.

Rob opened the jail cell and clipped the keys back to his belt. Ben noticed the blood on Rob's cuff and fought the panic triggered by the uncertainty of his daughter's wellbeing.

"Where is Nanshe?" Ben clenched his teeth to keep from saying more.

Chief Bowlin's eyes widened in feigned surprise, "Nanshe? Is that the name of your favorite ewe? Baaaa." He laughed under his breath which triggered a raspy cough.

"My daughter." Ben forced the words through gritted teeth.

"Oh, you have a daughter? I had no idea, but that might explain why that wife of yours fought so, so hard to break loose."

Ben raised a fist with intent of breaking the man's jaw, but Rob intercepted it and slammed Ben's wrist against the cell door instead. Ben could hear the bones snap but had little time to process the pain before he found himself face down on the concrete floor. Rob was sitting on his legs and had already snapped the handcuffs on so tightly that his broken wrist shot bolts of agony up to his elbow. It throbbed, but not as much as Ben's head pulsed with venomous outrage.

Rob stood up while saying, "Son of a bitch, try to hit me again and see what happens." He kicked Ben in the side, missing his kidney but catching a rib. "We're ending this once and for all. This is how it's going to go, are you listening to me, boy?" A second kick landed on the same rib. Rob laughed as he pushed his boot onto Ben's spine, keeping him on the floor. "Tell me how you like this story, son. We came to your house at 8:00 to arrest you and found your house on fire. We ran in to save your mama and baby, but they were already dead. You set the barn on fire and ran out shooting, killed some of the neighbors who showed up to kindly help put out the fire. Before we could stop you, you ran into the house and burned up to nothing. Bye-bye to the Black Whitmers. Grand Saline will talk about that crazy, murdering Black man for generations. Only we know ain't none of y'all Whitmers are kin, really. Every one of you's an abomination."

Ben didn't move or make a sound, but tears ran from his eyes at the thought of Nanshe being dead and her body burning to nothing. The thought engulfed him in hopelessness. He felt numb as Rob landed another kick into his side. Ben turned, curling his legs up in protection. He opened his eyes to see the door left standing wide open, a seemingly brighter light coming through. In the center of the doorway stood a different silhouette. A woman in a short, sheer gown held a shotgun. Rhoda. His heart shattered to see that Nanshe was not with her.

21

Rhoda's footsteps were as good as silent. No one could hear her over Police Chief Rob Bowlin planting his foot into Ben's body with such violent grunting that one would have thought Rob himself was being injured. She approached Rob from behind, the shotgun held in steady aim at his head. He did not see her.

"Get up now, boy!" Rob bent down and jerked Ben's arm causing his wrist to tug painfully against the handcuffs. "Get up and walk!"

Ben forced his eyes to the floor; he was terrified he might look at Rhoda and draw Rob's attention to her. He tried to hold off the inevitable while knowing things were about to get much worse. The thought entered his mind that Rhoda might be to blame for whatever happened at his farm, even for what was happening now. She should have kept Nanshe safe. She should have left him be. He could have taken care of his own self. Now she was going to get them all killed.

After Ben pulled his legs up under himself, he pushed his aching body to stand shakily before Rob Bowlin. The police chief sneered and wiped the corners of his mouth with his fingers, perhaps out of habit. His head tilted back a little as he eyed Ben like a butcher assessing a freshly killed boar.

"Once we get my brother's body loaded in the car," Rob whispered, "And I'm driving you back, I'm going to tell you what I did to her." He pulled his gun from his holster and pushed it up against the skin beneath Ben's chin. "I'm going to tell you what we all did to her until you break, boy. I'm going to break--"

The sound of Rhoda pumping the shotgun to load a shell in the chamber caused Rob to spin around, alarmed. He found himself looking directly down the barrel and into Rhoda's piercing glare. His mouth hung open in shock as he tried to find words, but all he could do was stammer incoherently.

"Drop your gun or I'll take your head off." Rhoda's voice was firm and hid the exhaustion she felt inside. She did not particularly want to shoot him. She just wanted him not to exist. She wanted him erased, all of the men in hoods erased, the entire week erased.

"Easy, little lady," Rob's voice shook as he tried to force a smile. He opened up his hand with the gun resting on his palm. "Take it if you want it."

"Drop it!" Rhoda screamed at him with such fury that his head jerked back. "Drop the goddamn gun!"

Rob let it fall and squeezed his eyes closed in fear it

would go off when it slammed onto the floor. It did not.

"Now, unlock the handcuffs."

Rob laughed nervously. "You come here to save this Negro? Do you even know what he's done? A woman of your kind should not be fooling around with no Black man."

"Unlock them or I'll search your dead body for the key."

Rob slowly moved his hand to his belt and took the key. Rhoda never took her eyes off him, ready to fire if he showed the least sign of aggression. She would not wait for a movement of hand. She was ready to destroy him if he even looked like he might attack her.

Ben's voice came gently, but Rhoda did not let it distract her. "Rhoda, what are you doing? What happened? Where is Nanshe?"

The handcuffs clicked unlocked. Ben winced in pain as Rob pulled the opened loops from around his broken wrist.

"Put your hands up!" Rhoda screamed at Rob. He immediately did as she said. His eyes darted around as he tried to come up with an escape plan. He hoped she would take Ben and leave, though it sickened him to think of them together in any way.

"Nanshe doesn't want me because I'm a killer," Rhoda said matter-of-fact to Ben without looking at him. "She won't drink. She needs you. She's in the office, asleep in a desk drawer. Take her and get her away from me. I don't want her to hear me kill again."

Ben's heart filled to bursting at the news that Nanshe was alive. He had doubted Rhoda, but she had come through. He wanted to wrap his arms around her in celebration, but thought it best he hold it back. Her eyes were trained on Rob. Ben looked at her now and saw the blood on her gown. He saw the blood in her hair. His heart wanted to pull himself away toward Nanshe, but a piece of it wanted to make things right by Rhoda. Whatever she had been through was partly-- perhaps mostly-- because of him. It must have been terrible. She deserved none of it.

"Go!" She shouted at Ben as if reading his mind; the burn of his pitying stare exhausted her even more.

At the startling sound of Rhoda's command, Nanshe woke and began to cry. Ben instinctively turned to go to her but paused when he saw Sheriff Creager emerge from the office with a bundled baby in one arm and a drawn pistol in his other. Nanshe kicked within the swaddled blanket and wailed. Rhoda's heart ached, wanting to go to her, wanting to turn and see how she had come into the room. But she held steady, her eyes and shotgun firmly aimed at Rob.

"Don't move you two!" Sheriff Creager called out. "There are ways to handle this by the law. I know you are innocent, Ben. Let's keep it that way!"

Rob responded with desperation, "She's trying to break this murderer out of jail!"

Rhoda gripped the shotgun and pressed it tighter against her shoulder in preparation to remove Rob's head. She glared at him in warning.

Sheriff Creager responded, "I understand you might have had something to do with that murder, Rob Bowlin. I'm here by a call from the governor. You are in a mess a trouble. But these two need to put down their weapons and let the law work."

Ben raised his hands to demonstrate he had no weapon. "I didn't know about any of this."

139

At the sound of Ben's voice, Nanshe screamed louder, more desperately. Tears filled Rhoda's eyes at the sound of it, but she held her stance.

"Is this your baby?" Sheriff Creager asked Ben.

"Yes."

"Get her out of here. Wait for us outside."

Ben moved quickly to take Nanshe from Sheriff Creager's arm before he changed his mind. Nanshe whimpered and became still at the touch of her father. Ben stared into the sheriff's eyes. "She's hurting. She's not bad. She's just hurting and needs some help, mental help."

It took a moment for the sheriff to understand Ben meant Rhoda, not the baby.

Ben continued, "Her baby died. She's suicidal. She needs help."

Sheriff Creager's mouth tightened with annoyance. He motioned for Ben to leave by nudging his head toward the front office. There was no indication that Ben had won any sympathy for Rhoda. But there was nothing more he could do. He walked away.

"Tell me what you want!" Sheriff Creager called out to Rhoda. "Nobody has to die."

Ben's heart tightened as he heard those words. Chills went up his spine as he understood that Rhoda had not come here just to save him. She wanted this to be the end. Sheriff Creager was her answered prayer, but Ben had one of his own. "Please don't kill her," Ben whispered his plea up to the office ceiling and beyond.

He stepped out the door into the night and met with a wisp of cold November air. A dead body lay just feet away. It was dressed in the obvious attire of the KKK. Ben suddenly felt more afraid to be there. If the death of that man had been blamed on him, the entire town would likely be after his head. This was no time for him, a Black man, to be outside at night.

He saw no sign of his truck but knew it must be somewhere nearby. Rhoda could not have just walked into town. But then he remembered how she had come to Grand Saline in the first place. He couldn't rule out anything with her. As much as he wanted to look for his truck to carry himself and Nanshe to safety, it was just too risky to go wandering around in the shadows.

His increasing paranoia was interrupted by the sound of a gunshot. There was no mistaking the sound of his own shotgun.

22

Ben ran back into the office but stopped short just beyond the door when he heard a second shot, this time from a handgun.

"No!"

He held Nanshe to his chest with her head cradled in his hand, pressed her comfortingly close, then charged into the jail. Sheriff Creager stood a few feet passed the entrance; his gun now pointed at the floor, held by a limp hand attached to a limp arm.

Sheriff Creager spoke in disbelief, "She shot him for no reason."

Rob Bowlin's body had slid down the jail cell door and came to rest in a seated position. The top of his head was completely gone. Blood splattered the walls behind him.

Rhoda had been shot from behind. She had fallen to her knees before toppling forward with the bullet from Sheriff Creager's handgun piercing her back. Blood bloomed out across the white of her gown.

Ben ran to her and tried to turn her over onto her back. He struggled to hold Nanshe steady. He winced at the pain in his wrist, but managed to flip her. Rhoda held her left hand over her stomach where the bullet had existed. Her right hand still remained loosely wrapped around the shotgun.

"No!" He screamed at the sight of the exit wound. "That was so stupid, Rhoda! That was so stupid! Why did you do this?"

Rhoda looked at him in a daze, "Because they have to pay."

"There will just be more of them. This didn't solve anything, Rhoda! It just got you killed!" He was crying, angry at her and pained by his biting sense guilt.

She smiled up at him now, her eyes finally focusing on Ben's irises. They looked so black in the shadows of the dimly lit jail. "It saved me the trouble," she whispered. "Thank you. Kiss her goodbye for me."

Her eyes fluttered and her mouth tightened in a spasm before her whole body relaxed. She was gone.

"Don't thank me!" Ben screamed at her. "Don't thank me! I didn't do this! I didn't have anything to do with this, dammit!" But it was a lie. He felt it in his heart, the guilt and shame of letting so many people down. And where was Paumina? Was she being burned alive as he wept over this stranger, this woman he had known for only two days? Was he losing his mind, too?

He hugged Nanshe closer and leaned over to press

his forehead to Rhoda's. His pent up grief flowed out of him as his tears fell into her eyes. He let himself cry for Della, too. The reality of the tragedy was too overwhelming to fight. He cried for himself and his powerlessness to change the past or even to simply walk out into the night to find his truck and drive home. The walls that had caged him in all his life were closing in too narrowly to be continually ignored. Who had he believed himself to be? Had he thought he could create internal peace in the center of such external belligerent hatred? He had been such a fool.

"We need to find your mother," came a voice from behind him. Sheriff Creager touched his shoulder, "I didn't know it was so bad here, son."

Ben suspected that was a lie. Everyone knew how bad it was in Grand Saline. Ben didn't want to go with the man who had shot Rhoda, even if Rhoda had given him little choice. But he needed to get home and he needed to find Paumina. Having someone with authority to protect him seemed cruelly necessary.

****

It may seem like fate that Paumina pulled up to the entrance of the farm only seconds after Sheriff Creager arrived with Ben. They had parked by the road. If she had been any earlier, she would have likely gone up to the house and been killed by the men milling about with torches and guns. Even Sheriff Creager refused to drive all the way up to the house. He stayed in his police car and hoped no one would recognize him.

The Sheriff, Ben, and Paumina stared ahead at the flames licking the sky. The men had not waited for Rob to return with Ben. They were not interested in destroying evidence; they simply wanted to destroy whatever was in front of them. The house had been lit on the western edge and the flames now danced along the roof.

"You shouldn't be here," Sheriff Creager said to Ben as if that was not obvious.

Ben found it ironic that those words would be said to him in relation to his own property. The men who should not be here were the men burning the place to the ground. But no one could stop it.

"My truck is in town. Take me there and we'll go." Ben felt numb.

"I can bring charges against these men in the morning. I'll gather my county officers and come back. We'll see to it that justice is served."

Again, Ben found humor in how Sheriff Creager believed his own lies. Or did he truly still believe in justice when it came to racism?

"Fine," Ben played along. "I'll ride with Paumina if you'll just follow us to find my truck. We'll go and let you do your job."

"Where will you go?"

Ben did not answer. He let the question hang in the air as it hung inside his mind. He didn't know. All he knew was that he could not bear to lose anything more.

Accepting that Ben had no plans to answer his question, Sheriff Creager backed his car up and turned it around. He pulled up beside Paumina's car. She sat behind the steering wheel, crying. Her mind was filled with thoughts of Benoni, the man who saved her, the man whose heart weighed in on every decision he had ever made. His legacy was gong up in flames.

Ben exited the police car and opened the driver's

side door of Paumina's car.

"We need to go. Hold Nanshe and I'll drive."

Paumina slid over to the right leaving her shoes kicked beneath the seat on the driver's side. She reached out to take Nanshe in her arms, hugged her with gratitude.

"Lord bless you, child." She looked down at the infant's puffy eyes, the result of hours of crying. "Lord bless you."

Epilogue

Nanshe, October 1988

All I knew of family was what existed southeast of Eldorado, Arkansas. They were Mama's family. I don't remember Mama at all, but I spent a lot of time with Mama's Mama. Sometimes I wished I had a real Mama, but most of the time I felt like Nana Bea was just as good as the real thing.

Daddy never said much about Mama, or much about anything else really. We had a small house on Nana Bea's farm but Daddy never saw much of it in the daylight. He worked for a lumber company and spent most of his time cutting down trees. When I was little, back before I even started school, Granny Mina would watch over me there. She was sick a lot, I remember that. And I remember the colors of her clothes, bright prints on silky fabrics. I remember thinking Granny Mina's clothes were magical. But I don't remember much else. She died in August of 1975, just a week before I started Kindergarten. On my first day of school I wore one of her scarves wrapped around my forehead so my natural curls were held up high. I remember believing I was magical, too.

I don't know why I didn't ask more questions. Life just kept going on and on. Daddy wasn't the only one working long hours. I never knew a time I didn't work, too. I worked at school, I worked to keep our house clean, I worked to pick berries and fruit in the orchards on Nana Bea's farm. I never expected it to get me anywhere because I never planned on going anywhere. I was fine right where I was. In hindsight, I think I worked so hard so I wouldn't have to think about ever leaving.

My uncles married local girls. I was in a lot of weddings. Some of them moved close by the farm. Some moved down to Louisiana or up to Tennessee. Nana Bea only had two daughters, one was my dead Mama and the other one never left the farm, seldom even left her room. Almost every time I saw her she was crying. Later I wondered if that was because I looked like Mama.

We only had one photo of Mama and Daddy together. It was taking on their wedding day. I never knew why Daddy didn't have more than that. I assumed Daddy was poor and didn't have money for photographs. I didn't find out I was wrong about that until Daddy died two weeks ago. He had a heart attack getting ready for work. I was an hour away in Louisiana at Grambling University. He wasn't found until the lumber company called Nana Bea's house. Jeanie answered and woke Nana. They called me before the sun rose, said to come home.

I should be back at Grambling now, but I told them I needed the semester off to get Daddy's affairs in order. I don't know why I thought I needed a whole semester to deal with what Daddy left behind. I really didn't think Daddy had "affairs" to "get in order". I just didn't want to leave home. I felt like I wasted so much time. I never questioned Daddy about his running and avoiding. You might think a man can't run away from something and be standing in the same place all the time. But, a man can. Daddy could. There was a space between us as wide as the Mississippi; but I ran from it, too. I knew it was bad, whatever happened to Mama. I knew there was a story Daddy didn't want to tell and that made me not want it told, too. I didn't push, but after Daddy died it didn't feel like pushing was the right word. Allow is the better term. I didn't allow it. Maybe he wanted to share his burden but

I never gave him space for it. I was too busy scrubbing down walls, crushing grapes for jelly, planting flowers from the porch ten feet out of the driveway. I was afraid to sit still a minute and allow the words to be said.

Going through my father's things was, obviously, not something I did while he was alive. If I couldn't bring myself to sit in stillness with the man himself, I certainly wasn't going to snoop through his belongings. Even after his death, I didn't want to do it. I asked Nana Bea to come down and help. She looked at me like I'd asked her to inspect a boil on my butt, like she would if there was absolutely no way to get out of it. I'm not one for making anybody do anything they don't want to do. I hugged Nana and told her it was okay, I could do it on my own. I made her believe it, too.

When I finally got to going through his dresser drawers the first thing I found was a blue zippered pouch. I opened it up and Lord Almighty at the money. I had seen a hundred dollar bill one time in my whole life. In that zippered pouch there was a fat stack of them and gold coins in the bottom, old ones I didn't recognize. I was so confused by it. We'd been eating fried bologna sandwiches and even canning up every salvageable part of worm eaten beans. I'd been given a single new dress every year and hadn't had a new pair of shoes in two. If not for my obsessive work ethic which earned me a scholarship, I'd never have even tried to go to college. We couldn't afford it. And yet all the while, we could. I felt lied to at the same time I felt blessed. I felt Daddy had denied me things at the same time I felt he had provided for me above and beyond anything I could have expected.

And then I found the letter he wrote. It was

addressed to me, dated January 1970. And that is why I am writing this down while I sit in a field of tall grass in Grand Saline, TX. That letter is why my back is propped up against the grave marker of Rhoda Evanson, a name I had never heard. I have read this letter aloud to Mama's grave just an arm's length from Rhoda's and she has yet to respond. There's not a thing but silence from either of these women unless they're speaking so low I can't hear.

I will not share with you the entire letter. But I will leave you with this excerpt:

"I find myself wishing she had come sooner. I imagine her walking up and saving Della to be a hero instead of the criminal she was after shooting the chief of police. But she didn't want to be hero. She wasn't trying to save me and I doubt she would have tried to save Della. She was trying to save you because she failed to save her own baby girl.

Seeing Rhoda die shouldn't have been so hard on me. But it just added to the tragedies I couldn't prevent. I had just lost your mother, my farm, my sheep, and I had a target on my own back. I had nothing left in Grand Saline and no way to ensure your safety there. I buried Rhoda by the treeline beside your Mama in what will soon become an overgrown prairie with large post oak trees. I pay my taxes so it won't be taken and given to the Crosswhites, but I'll never step foot there again. I hope you never go there, either. But if you're reading this because I died, please don't sell the farm just yet. One day, maybe by the time you have grandchildren, the town might have earned forgiveness. One day, maybe our family can rebuild."

A Note from the Author

Silencer was created to delve into the complicated nature of suicidal thoughts. When are they a coping mechanism and when are they dangerous? Is there a difference?

Grand Saline, TX became the setting of this novel because of Charles Robert Moore, a United Methodist Minister who grew up in Grand Saline in the 1940's and 1950's, witnessed the racism, and returned to the town in 2014 in an attempt to right the wrongs done by the citizens of the town. He was 79 years old when he set himself on fire at a shopping center in Grand Saline. He left behind a typed, two page suicide note explaining why he had done it, what he had witnessed as a young man, and why it was so important for him to give his life to end the racism and the harm done to Blacks in Grand Saline.

I found his suicide note to be very moving. I was surprised by how thoughtful and deliberate it was considering the horrific nature of what he was about to do to himself. All he wanted was to awaken in others the passion to right history's wrongs. I believe he thought his suicide would matter. I believe he weighed the pain of self-immolation and the effect it would have on our hearts and he decided the pain was worth it.

But a month after setting himself on fire, there were very few newspapers that had reported the story. I was able to find three. Two of them treated it as a spectacle of insanity. The third was more balanced.

I don't believe self-immolation is a solution to racism. I don't believe the words of Charles Robert Moore prompted more change after his suicide than he could have brought about with a couple more decades of speaking aloud about the issue. I wish he had not died. But I do not think it's fair to portray him as a raving madman at the expense of his cause.

We often misuse terms for mental illness and the idea of mental illness itself. We define things as "crazy" which are weird or criminal or over-the-top. We minimize the real effects of mental illness by attaching its words to these things for amusement. This is harmful to those with real diagnoses in need of real medical care. I hoped in writing Silencer to bring attention to the nuances of depression and suicidal ideation as well as racism in the south. I hope readers are satisfied with the portrayal or are at least left contemplative.

Other Books by Julie Roberts Towe:

Winter Seedlings

Winter Suns

Hold This Close
(prequel to Winter Seedlings)

The Departed

www.ingramcontent.com/pod-product-compliance
Lightning Source LLC
Chambersburg PA
CBHW070933130626
46555CB00001B/407